# ALWAYS ROOM FOR CUPCAKES

Delilah Horton, Book 1

BETHANY LOPEZ

Want to learn more about my books? Sign up for my newsletter and Join my
FB Group/Street Team!
https://landing.mailerlite.com/webforms/landing/r7w3w5
https://www.facebook.com/groups/1443318612574585/

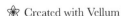 Created with Vellum

*I would like to give a shout out, and say "thank you", to Heather Hildenbrand. A smart, savvy writer, businesswoman, and mentor of authors, who I am proud to call a friend. Always giving and inspirational, I'm so happy to have her in my life.*

# Prologue

One day you're be-bopping along, jamming to the music in your head while wondering if your thighs can handle grabbing a cupcake on the way home. The next thing you know your entire world crashes and burns.

I used to wake up at night in a sweat, crying because I'd dreamt that my husband was cheating on me, or that he hated me and resented our kids. He'd always hold me close and tell me it was all just a dream, that he loved me and our family and he'd never let us go.

He was a fucking liar.

Instead of being the sweet, affable, hard-working man he projected to me and the outside world, he was actually a cheating, vagina-licking asshole who only cared about getting off and being free of responsibility.

I'd gone from a sweet and caring housewife to bitter, hard-as-nails single mom, who worked her ass off to give her kids a quarter of the life they were used to. Putting my photography skills to use, I'd gone to work for a scumbag PI. He used me to dig up dirt on his clients.

I was happy to do it.

I was doing a public service for women like me who thought the men in their lives could actually be trusted and I *really* enjoyed my job.

I'd learned quickly that men suck, my children are my saving grace, and there is *always* room for cupcakes.

# Chapter 1

"Get it in focus this time, Lila ... none of that grainy shit you sent me last week. I need to actually see what's going down, or in this case, what's entering what."

"Ugh, thanks for the mental image, Moose," I said with a grimace into my cell. "It's bad enough I have to see that shit through my lens, I don't need you constantly talking about it."

"Quit your bitchin' and get me some good shots. This one's a high roller."

"Got it, boss," I replied, and pressed *end* on the call.

My boss may be a creepy, low-life PI, but he'd taken a chance on me when my douchebag ex left me high and dry. So even though I regularly gave him shit, he knew I'd do anything for him.

Especially if that meant a more lucrative paycheck.

That's why I was currently scrunched down in my caravan outside a seedy hotel, a half-eaten sandwich on my lap and my camera at the ready.

Moose got the clients, then hired me to get the goods. This usually involved taking pictures of men and women having affairs. But sometimes it was as easy as following them and snapping a shot of them being somewhere they weren't supposed to be.

Being a wronged woman myself, I didn't feel guilty about catching liars and cheaters in the act. I just wish I'd had an inkling there were problems in my own marriage and had thought to hire someone like Moose and me to get evidence against *The Douche.*

*Instead, I'd been clueless.*

I thought my twelve-year marriage was perfect. I'd been a doting housewife who'd loved raising our kids, keeping the house spic and span and having a hot meal ready for our family dinners every night. My husband made good money, we had a nice house, and we lived in a neighborhood where the kids could play outside and we didn't have to worry about their safety.

Then one day he was supposed to be out with his buddies watching the game at a local bar, when Elena, one of our twins, had a sharp pain in her stomach that wouldn't quit. I got scared and tried to call him but he didn't answer. Since our town was small enough that I could drive around it in fifteen minutes, I packed the kids in the car and went to the bar.

Imagine my surprise when neither he nor his buddies were there. Figuring I got the place wrong, I activated the phone finder app I'd installed on all of our phones and ended up in the parking lot behind Starbucks.

Seeing some movement in his car, I told the kids I'd be right back and jogged over to the vehicle, which, although it didn't register at the time, had foggy windows.

Filled with worry over our daughter I didn't think, I just acted, and yanked the car door open. That's when I saw Slutty Shirley Finkle, legs spread wide, bare cunt lifted in the air, with *my* husband's face buried nose deep inside.

"*You mother-fucking son of a whore!*"

Yup, I'm pretty sure those were the exact words I'd yelled in the Starbucks parking lot before snapping a picture with my phone and hightailing it out of there to get my daughter to the hospital.

Now, my kids and I lived in a shitty three-bedroom apartment in The Heights. I worked for Moose and picked up shifts at my best friend, Amy May's bakery whenever I could. They saw their dad most weekends while *I* avoided him at all costs.

He'd humiliated me, broken my trust, and made me feel like an idiot for having such blind faith in him all of those years. I hated everything about him. His blond wavy hair, his chiseled jaw, and the stupid way he looked in a perfectly tailored suit. I wanted no reminder of the life we had together, except for our beautiful children of course, which was why I'd left all of our material possessions behind with him in the house we'd once shared.

As I watched a slick-looking middle aged man guide a heavily breasted, much younger woman into the seedy motel, I thought, *this one's for the sisterhood*. I pumped my fist as I watched them walk back out of the office and down a few doors, then got ready to strike.

First floor … nice. At least this time I wouldn't have to climb anything.

When I'd first started out about ten months ago, I'd been woefully out of shape. After being chased down the street by a heavyset woman wearing only a teddy and almost getting tackled, I'd decided it would be in my best interest to join a gym and take up running.

It made all the difference. Sometime I had to get creative, but, *knock on wood*, I always got the shot … even if it was sometimes grainy.

Taking pictures of people in the act is actually easier than you might think. People are stupid. Especially the ones who think they're untouchable, they'll never get caught, and their shit don't stink.

I eased out of the van, looking around the mostly empty parking lot as I walked casually toward the door they'd entered. I even started whistling just to make myself more inconspicuous.

*Hiding in plain sight actually worked.*

"Thanks for leaving the curtains cracked," I murmured as I slid up to the window, camera up and ready, and peeked inside.

Unfortunately for me, but fortunately for my pocketbook, they'd left the lights blaring and must have done some heavy petting in the car because they were already going at it.

"Sixty-nine … *classic*."

I snapped quickly, making sure their faces were in frame as I captured each lick, suck, slobber, and moan.

"*Gross*," I grumbled as I hurried back to my car.

One of the downsides of the job was that it sometimes took hours to get the sordid visions out of my head. On occasions like these, there was one thing that helped ease my pain.

*I needed a cupcake.*

# Chapter 2

"You're a genius," I moaned as the chocolaty goodness hit my tongue.

Amy May was on the other side of the counter pouring me a steaming cup of coffee as I made love to one of her cupcakes from a cherry-red stool on the other side.

Amy May was a Midwestern girl who'd married her high school sweetheart, Jason, and traveled with him when he joined the military. She'd always had a love of sweets and had picked the brains of bakers all over the world. Amy May had fused everything she loved into one kick-ass idea and opened her bakery on Main Street. Even if she didn't own the only bakery in town, her diner-inspired motif coupled with her assortment of French, Italian, and Polish pastries, in addition to her sinfully delicious cupcakes, made her the town treasure she is.

"Rough morning?"

"You have no idea," I said with an eye roll, popping the last bit of cake in my mouth. "I'll spare you the gory details."

"What else you got on tap today?" she asked, pulling her shoulder-length, dirty-blonde hair back into a small tail at the nape of her neck.

"Headed to the library to shoot these pics over to Moose, then see if I can get a line on this chick who's been supposedly working for Clarice's Nail Salon. The husband says no money ever comes in ... Should be pretty low-key."

"Kids with you?"

"Yeah. They don't go to *The Douche's* until Friday this week."

"You wanna come over for dinner?"

"Nah, it's burger night at Casa Horton, but I'll take a rain check."

"Sounds good, babe, see you tomorrow."

"Yeah," I replied, standing up and picking up my trash. I'd tried to pay my bill when Amy May's had first opened only to be told I got the best friend discount for life.

It's a good thing I'd found exercise, or my ass would be the size of a house. As it is, it's only about the size of a singlewide.

"Thanks, girl."

Amy May gave me a little wave, then blew me a kiss and I was gone.

Rather than drive twenty minutes to my place in The Heights, I usually worked out of the Greenswood Public Library. It was only a couple blocks from Amy May's and was a nice quiet place to do what I needed to do.

"Hey, Clare," I called, keeping my voice loud enough for her to hear the greeting, but low enough so she wouldn't shush me.

Clare had been working the desk at the library since the first time I'd stepped foot in it to check out Shel Silverstein's *Where the Sidewalk Ends*. I'd been eight and could have sworn Clare was a hundred.

She still looked exactly the same.

I wandered through the aisles, back to the workstation I'd claimed as my own, and logged in. After sending Moose the pictures, I checked my email, then signed off.

Moose's "office" was actually his screened-in back porch, so I tried to keep all of our communication over the phone and through email, only going to his place if it was absolutely necessary. Not to say that I didn't feel safe around my boss or anything; he was just a little creepy, so I felt better with things this way.

Moose shot me a text saying he got the photos and he'd just driven by the nail salon and saw our next perp's car.

Now, I'm not a cop, and the clients aren't always correct in their accusations, but still, I had to call the people we were spying on *something*, so I called them perps. I sure as shit wasn't going to remember all of their names so *perp* was just easier. Plus, I thought it made my job sound cooler, like I was actually doing something that made a difference.

Ater reading the text, I turned on my heel and headed down the street toward Clarice's, wishing I'd worn sneakers instead of my boots today. I'd gone for style rather than comfort, which was never the smart choice, but the boots paired with my skinny jeans and long pullover sweater looked much better than sneakers.

"Hey, Lila," Clarice said in greeting when I walked inside.

"What's up, Clarice?"

"Same shit different day."

"I hear that," I replied.

See, although my town was small, I'd managed to keep a lid on my side job. The town loved to talk. And with the way I'd caught my husband and Slutty Shirley Finkle, promptly left my cushy home in The Woods for a shitty apartment in The Heights, then started working for my best friend... they had plenty to talk about when the subject of me came up.

This was good for me and for Moose because it meant people never suspected when I was around that there was a possibility I was looking into them. I didn't know how long that shit would last, but I'd been lucky so far ...

*No one really suspects a single mother of twins who drives a minivan and has an ongoing love affair with cupcakes to be sneaking around and capturing their bad deeds on camera.*

I looked around the salon and, not seeing the perp, I walked up to Clarice and whispered, "Can I use your bathroom? Sorry to bust in since I don't have an appointment, but I think I just started my period."

"Yeah, girl, of course."

"Thanks," I said sheepishly, then pushed through the curtain into the back room.

I tiptoed quietly, pulling my camera out of my oversized Coach purse, one of the few things left over from my previous life.

Keeping my eyes peeled and my ears open, I searched the back.

A sniffling sound had me turning right. I peeked around the corner just in time to see my perp bending over a table, getting ready to snort the three lines of coke she had cut out.

I'd spent an entire day trying out different cameras until I'd finally found one that didn't make a sound when a picture was taken and still came out with quality images. That meant I could lift my camera, get my shot, and be gone without the cokehead even realizing I'd been there.

After I got a couple shots, I decided it was best to sneak out the back rather than show my face in the storefront again. I slowly pushed the back door open and eased out.

"*Who the fuck are you?*"

I whipped my head up as I was shoving the camera back in my purse and saw a strange man standing by a rehabbed old Camaro, smoking a cigarette.

"Uh … a friend of Clarice's. I was just using the bathroom," I managed, not sure who the guy was or what my next move should be.

"Yeah?" he asked, throwing his cigarette to the ground and taking a step toward me. "You need a camera to do that?"

*Shit.*

Before he could make another move, I secured my bag on my shoulder, turned and took off like a shot.

I hit Main Street, cursing myself for wearing the damn boots when the sound of a motorcycle pulling up along side of me caused me to turn my head.

My first thought was, *where the hell did the bike come from?*

Then I realized it wasn't the slimy guy from behind the salon. The bike came to a stop and the most dangerously beautiful man I'd ever seen rumbled, "Get your sweet ass on the bike."

*Huh?*

I stood there for a moment, wondering what in the hell was happening, if I should get on this strange man's bike, and if I was offended or flattered by his *sweet ass* comment.

"*Darlin'*," he prodded.

I turned my head to look behind me and saw the slimy guy standing at the side of Clarice's and made a quick decision to accept … *his offer of a ride and the compliment.* So, I swung my leg up and over the bike, settled my front to his back, and curled my arms around the thick bulk of his muscled body.

Tingling head to toe from the adrenaline and the close contact with a seriously hot man, I couldn't stop my lips from spreading into a grin as we took off down Main Street.

# Chapter 3

As we came to a stop at a park outside of town, I was subtly inhaling the scent of leather and spice and wondering how the hell I'd ended up here.

Funnily enough, I wasn't scared. I didn't feel a vibe that said he intended to hurt me in any way. Mostly I was curious, and, if I was honest, a little turned on.

Once the bike came to a complete stop, I reluctantly got off but had to keep one hand on the seat while my legs stopped shaking.

"Uh … thanks," I mumbled as he kicked the stand down and turned his dark eyes to me.

*Are they black? Is it even possible to have black eyes?*

Everything about him was dark. His eyes, his hair, his deeply tanned skin. He wore a trimmed beard, which only added to his dangerous look, and had what looked like shoulder-length wavy hair, which was pulled back off of his face. Paired with motorcycle boots, jeans that fit like a glove, and a black leather jacket, the man was a billboard for raw male sexuality.

"Anytime, darlin'," he said with a small smirky smile. "I've seen you around."

"Huh?" I asked, apparently having lost my ability to speak in actual words.

"I've seen you around... on the job, so I've kept my eye out."

*Crap!* Did he mean he knew I was spying on people? I guess I wasn't as covert as I thought I was.

"*Shit!*" I muttered, then wondered how the hell he'd seen me, when I'd never seen him before in my life.

"Don't worry your cover's still good. I've only seen you, 'cause I've been looking."

"You have?"

"Yeah. I saw you a couple weeks ago, walking down Main, and I gotta say, one look and I knew I wanted to see more ... So I've been paying attention. Those assholes you follow are more worried about getting into whatever trouble they can find, than paying attention to some hot mom in her soccer van. You gotta be careful though, darlin', a light as bright as yours won't be hidden for long."

"You saw me a couple weeks ago?" I asked, still stuck on that, not yet ready to think about my bright light.

He nodded. "Then again at the motel on sixth, in the parking lot of the Applebee's, and going into the bakery with your kids. Gotta say, that last time you were walking and laughing with your kids and when your blue eyes hit me as you were going inside, I *knew* ... I've been waiting for an opportunity. Got one today."

I was wearing shades, so his description of my eyes meant he had, in fact, seen me before, but as I looked him over I didn't know how that was possible.

"I don't remember you and *I* gotta say, I think I'd remember."

That earned me a grin as he replied, "You were out with your kids, so you weren't paying attention. I was."

Hmmmm.

"What's your name?" I asked, finally getting to what probably should have been the first thing out of my mouth.

"Cade."

"I'm Lila," I said, lamely holding out my hand.

"Delilah Horton," he said, taking my hand and bringing it to his lips and I could have sworn I felt the brush of his facial hair all over my skin.

"You want my job?" I half joked, surprised he knew my name. I wondered how a man like him could have been looking into me and I'd had no idea.

Cade chuckled.

"Nah, I'll leave you to it. Now, I gotta know ... I've seen you alone, with your girl, and with your kids. No ring." He looked pointedly down at my hand. "You got a man?"

I'm sure my eyes were wide and my face was covered in shock, that's how taken aback I was at his question. Sure, he'd said he'd seen me around and even I wasn't so dense I didn't notice the flirting, but I'd never had a guy pursue me before. Not like this.

With *The Douche*, I was the instigator. The only other serious boyfriend I'd had before him was in high school, which pretty much entailed him asking me if I wanted to sit with him at lunch and *Bam!* We were dating.

I was unsure what to make of Cade, but I realized I'd only been with him for a short amount of time and he definitely lit a fire in my belly ... along with other places ... so I mentally shrugged and thought, *what could it hurt?* It's not like I was going to take him home, introduce him to my kids, and we were all going to move in together.

Maybe a walk on the wild side was just what I needed.

So I replied, "Nope, no man. Just an ex." Then I mimicked

him and looked down at his hand and asked, "What about you? No ring ... no woman?"

"Not if I'm with you," he stated.

I wasn't sure how I felt about that answer, but right then my phone went off, distracting me from questioning him further.

"I gotta get back," I said after I read the text.

Cade gave me a brief nod, then righted the bike and kicked the stand back up, scooting forward to give me room to get back on.

I may have hugged him a smidge tighter than necessary and taken advantage of the closeness to allow my senses to get their fill of him.

The ride was over much quicker than I liked, but I got off when he stopped in front of the bakery and said, "Thanks for saving my ass back there."

He just lifted his chin slightly and stated, "I want you on my bike tomorrow. We'll grab dinner."

My heart leapt in my throat.

"Uh, I can't tomorrow, I've got my kids," I replied, then quickly added before I could think better of it, "But, they're with their dad this weekend."

"Friday, then."

When he looked like he was about to leave I asked, "Don't you need to know where I live?"

Cade just shot me a look, then took off, the sounds of his motorcycle growing distant as I watched him get farther and farther away.

"What the hell?" I whispered, then turned my head and laughed when I saw Amy May standing behind the counter, her mouth wide open as she stared out at me.

I kept laughing out loud, like a freak on the street, and gave her a little wave as I walked away.

My phone rang immediately.

"Get your ass back here and tell me *who the hell that was*," Amy May screeched in my ear before I could even say hello.

"I'll call you later," I managed, still laughing.

"No, you can't do this to me…" I heard her yell as I ended the call.

And as I walked to my car, smiling and chuckling softly to myself I realized I felt lighter, and giddier, than I had in years.

# Chapter 4

"What are you so happy about?"

I looked over my shoulder at my ten-year-old daughter who was standing behind me in the kitchen, tablet in hand, her headphones down around her neck.

"Just a good day," I replied, before turning back to the cutting board and resuming singing along with the Top 40 music playing in the background.

When I didn't get a response, or hear any movement, I turned back to see Elena still standing there watching me curiously.

*Shit*, had it been that long since I'd been in a good mood?

"Everything okay?" I asked.

Elena shrugged and answered, "Yeah, I guess," then put her headphones back on and walked out of the room.

The twins had come home, finished their homework, and retreated to their separate bedrooms to *do their thing* before dinner. This typically meant Elena was on her tablet and Elin was sitting in his gaming chair playing video games online while talking to his friends through his headphones.

After dinner the drill was family time, showers, then back to their lairs for a little private time before bed.

This worked for us since we enjoyed being around each other, but really liked our private time too. It also meant minimal bickering between the twins, who were really close, but were still ten-year-old kids, which meant they got on each other's nerves.

I finished up the potato salad and went to pull the burgers off the grill. It was homemade burger night, so there was a bacon cheddar burger for Elena, feta and spinach burger for me, and a plain hamburger with season salt for Elin. It was a night of family favorites, paired with the potato salad and grilled asparagus, and something we had at least every other week.

I grabbed the kids so we could sit at the table and eat as a family, which is what we did every night they were with me. I may not be able to give them the things we had when I was married to their father, but I could give them a home-cooked meal and family time.

That's what I'd had growing up and I thought it was an important tradition to keep.

"Dad said we're going camping this weekend," Elena said, effectively dropping a bomb in my lap.

My fork clattered against my plate as I dropped it and asked, "Say what?"

"Camping," Elena repeated.

"Your dad doesn't go camping," I explained. And he didn't. He was the opposite of outdoorsy.

"Well, when I told him that Carl's parents bought an RV and go camping all the time and I wanted to try it, he went out and bought one." This was said by Elin.

"He bought an RV? What the hell?"

"Swear jar," Elin shot out.

In an effort to get the kids not to swear, *The Douche* and I had introduced the swear jar. Anytime someone swore, they had to put a quarter in the jar and every so often we'd cash it out and the kids would get to pick out a movie to watch at the theater or we'd go out for ice cream. I'd put a lot of money in that jar since the divorce. Elin loved that damn thing.

"Mom, *yeah*, we're going camping in Dad's new RV." This Elena said quietly.

I took a moment to look around the room, then gave myself a small pinch to make sure I was awake.

"You *mentioned* that one of your friends had an RV and you wanted to *try* it, so your dad went out and *bought* one?"

The twins were now watching me like they were afraid my head might explode. And they were right … it was about to.

*That son of a bitch*, I shouted in my head, while trying to keep my face blank for the kids' sake. *Throwing money around on stupid shit, shit I could never in a million years compete with…*

"Mom?" Elin called tentatively. "Are you gonna blow a gasket?"

Deciding it was best to change the subject I asked, "Your friend's name is Carl? Who names their kid Carl nowadays?"

"Uh, yeah, not everyone has weird names like us," Elin said.

"Your names aren't weird," I argued.

"Yes, they are," Elena put in.

"Are not."

"I've never met another Elin in *my whole life…*"

"You're ten, give it time," was my response.

They shot me identical looks that screamed, "*Whatever*" then took bites of their burgers.

Sometimes it was a little freaky when they did things in sync like that, without even realizing it.

We stayed away from mentions of RVs and Carl for the rest of dinner. When we were done, Elena did the dishes and Elin took out the trash, before leaving me alone to check in on my computer and see if there were any new developments from Moose.

Moose had responded back to my shots of the cokehead and told me I'd gotten what he wanted. But, since this was the first actual *illegal* activity I'd captured, I didn't feel right just leaving it at that.

*I should probably give copies to Bea,* I thought.

Beatrice "Bea" Cooper was a local cop and my other best friend. She wasn't in love with my new profession, but appreciated it when I kept her in the loop with stuff happening in Greenswood.

Moose had also sent me info on a new job, so it looked like tomorrow would be a full day. I'd have to stop by the police station on the way to Amy May's, put in a few hours at the bakery, then head to the bank to try and get some dirt on one of the tellers.

This made me sigh ... loudly, because *The Douche* was the Branch Manager at the bank I'd be staking out. Not only did I not want to be that close to him unless absolutely necessary, but he also didn't know what I did to pick up extra money and I didn't want him to.

Not that I thought working with Moose put my kids in any danger, or affected them at all, but I worried my ex might have other ideas.

He may be a cheating bastard, but he was a great dad and he might have objections about me following around the underbelly of Greenswood, The Heights, and the next three counties.

# Chapter 5

"Have you ever seen the guy behind Clarice's anywhere before?" Bea asked after I told her what I'd seen the day before.

"No," I replied with a shake of my head. "And I'm sure I'd remember… he was pretty slimy."

"Okay, I'll talk to Clarice and see if she knows who he is," Bea replied, then she cocked her head and looked at me seriously. "I need you to be careful, Lila. I've been pretty quiet about you working for Moose." I almost snorted at that, because she'd made her feelings on the matter *very* clear. "But if this guy's some sort of drug dealer or something from out of town he probably won't take too kindly to you taking pictures and talking to the cops."

"I hear you; if I see him again I'll steer clear."

"And give me a call."

"And give you a call," I promised.

Bea may be petite, with a pixie cut and tiny features, but she could take down a man twice her size in minutes. I'd seen it happen and it was *awesome*!

"I gotta get to Amy May's," I said, gathering my things as I stood. "You gonna stop by to get coffee this morning?"

"Nah, Shannon made me breakfast and sent me with a to-go cup," she replied, gesturing to her mug that said, *I am woman, so back the fuck off.*

"Nice," I said with a laugh. "All right then, Bea, I'll see ya later."

"Bye, babe," Bea said, then called out before I could get to the door, "Watch your back."

I gave her a thumbs up, then exited the station and climbed in my van so I could get to work.

"You didn't call me and you didn't answer my texts," Amy May accused before the door of the bakery had even closed behind me.

"I know, I'm sorry. I was busy with the kids, then work and was just so wiped I ended up going to sleep early. I knew I'd be here this morning, so I figured you'd be all right with me telling you in person."

Amy May was quiet for a moment, then threw her hands up, exasperated.

"*Well … Who was the sex god on the bike?*"

Kidding around, I covered my ears at her screech and yelled, "Sheesh… don't yell!"

My best friend rounded the corner, her finger wagging.

"Don't play games with me, Delilah Horton, or I'll tell Elena how you kissed Joey Miller on the lips under the bleachers when we were eleven. How old is she again?"

"*Easy,*" I replied throwing up my hands, knowing full well Amy May always followed through on her threats. "I'll tell you…"

So I told her all of it: the cokehead, the slimy guy behind Clarice's, and Cade pulling up next to me and helping me out of a bad situation. Then I told her about the date.

"You're going to go out with him?" She made a point of looking me up and down and before repeating, "*You?*"

"Hey, what does that mean?" I asked, crossing my arms over my chest.

"It means that both," Amy May held up two fingers, as if I didn't understand what *both* meant, "Joey Miller and The Douche are a certain *type* of guy. Clean cut, bordering on metrosexual, pretty boys, who wouldn't know how to give a girl a *wild ride* if she gave them play-by-play instructions ... But that *man* you were with yesterday? He could give a girl an orgasm just by looking at her. He is the opposite of your usual pretty boys. I didn't know you had it in you."

Although I was slightly offended, I had to admit she had a point.

But still... "Did you *see* him? I don't know if you got a good enough look, because if you had you'd know I really had no choice. He's that freaking hot! And, manly? I've always prided myself on being a good role model for women, but if Cade wanted to hit me over the head with a club, throw me over his shoulder, then take me off and ravage me .... I'd give him the club."

Amy May nodded, her eyes wide in a way I knew even though she loved her husband, Jason, she'd like to be clubbed by Cade as well.

A little more seriously, I added, "I don't know, Amy May, I know he's different. A little dangerous, overbearing, maybe a little scary even, but *God,* I haven't felt that way with a man in ... *ever.* I think I owe it to myself to see what happens, even if it just ends up being a crazy mistake."

"I agree."

"You do?"

"Absolutely, girl, you deserve this. After everything you've been through you deserve to have a man who'll fuck you like it's *his job*."

I giggled at that, slapping my hand over my mouth at the girlish act.

"C'mon, let's get to work." She put her arm around my shoulder and led me around the corner. "You have to promise to tell me everything. No more teasing or making me wait. I don't care if he's just rolled off you and hasn't even taken off the condom yet, *you call me*."

"I swear it," I said, looking down at her offered pinky and wrapping it with mine.

# Chapter 6

I stood outside the bank, the scenario I'd come up with working through my brain.

I couldn't believe I was going to do this but I had to have a justifiable reason for being in the bank I'd left at the same time I'd left my ex.

I'd seen the perp inside but knew the only way I'd be able to get close enough to see her and maybe speak with her, would be to finally give *The Douche* the confrontation he'd been looking for.

Ugh, I felt like I needed a shower just *thinking* about going into his office and having this conversation, but Moose needed this girl and I needed the money, so...

Like every other time I'd walked into this bank during our marriage, as soon as I crossed the threshold, *The Douche's* eyes found mine, as if his gut told him anytime I was on the premises.

I used to think it was romantic, like we were drawn to each other or something, now it just pissed me off. Like everything else about him...

He rose from behind his desk and went to the door to his office, waiting and watching curiously as I beelined for him.

Being in that glass box all day would have driven me crazy, but he liked it. I think it made him feel more powerful, validated his status in some way.

"Delilah," he said cautiously, probably worried I'd make a scene. Which, honestly, was always a possibility whenever we were breathing the same air.

"*Douche*," I replied with an evil grin.

"*Jesus, Lila*, not here," he said under his breath, his hand coming out to grab my forearm and drag me into his office.

I was about to rip my arm away when he released it, shutting the glass door behind us.

I positioned myself so I was standing between him and his desk, my perp directly in my line of sight in her position at the counter.

"What are you doing here?"

"You've been saying that you wanted to 'explain' for the last ten months," I began, my hands on my hips in an angry stance that wasn't only for effect. "Well, now I'm ready to hear it."

*The Douche* ran his hand through his perfectly coifed locks, messing them up unintentionally and I had a little jolt of glee that he'd be annoyed later when he realized he'd gone through his workday rumpled.

*I never said I wasn't a bitch.* I had to be, to come to his job this way, staging a confrontation I in no way wanted to have, in order to have eyes on my perp ... for a measly picture worth a hundred dollars.

*Oh well, I'd already gone too far to back out now.*

He cleared his throat and brought his pained eyes to mine.

"It was a mistake, Lila, a one-time fuck-up that ruined my life. I'm sorry and I regret it every day."

My heart started to bleed at his words, so I hardened it,

crossing my arms over my chest and asking, "Really? That's it? That's all you've been wanting to tell me? All the texts and phone calls... telling the kids you needed to talk..."

"I never should have said anything to the kids," he said, his chiseled jaw clenching. "But I *am* sorry, babe."

"No, you don't get to call me babe anymore. If it was such a mistake, how did it happen? We were married for twelve damn years ... How could you accidentally end up with your face in Slutty Shirley Finkle's snatch behind the *fucking* Starbucks? That shit doesn't just happen. You're saying it was your only time with her?'

*The Douche* stepped closer, his five-foot-nine frame only slightly taller than my five-foot-seven one, so we could almost see eye to eye.

"We weren't the same," he said, and I knew he was talking about us. About the last couple years of our marriage. "You were busy with the kids and your events at school and I was working all the time. It seemed like when I was home, you didn't have time for me, so I wasn't in a hurry to *be* home. We weren't talking, we weren't having sex, shit, we barely even touched each other..."

I held up a hand to stop him, teetering on the brink of rage or tears, I wasn't sure which, maybe both. I faced the floor, trying to keep my mask in place.

"I've had a lot of time to think over the past ten months and I can accept that the issues in our marriage were because of both of us. We both knew things weren't great, but we didn't talk about it and we didn't work out how to fix it. I'll give you that."

Then I looked into his handsome face and at his flinch, I knew the pain was apparent on mine.

"What I can't forgive is your absolute lack of respect for me. Not for the mother of your kids, or the woman who kept your home, for *me ... your wife*. If you were tempted you should have talked to me, or at the very least, told me you wanted to separate, get a divorce. Maybe that would have shaken us up enough to get some help, but to *cheat* … That shows not only did you not respect me, but you didn't love me either. Because if you did, you wouldn't hurt and humiliate me that way. *In a fucking parking lot.*"

I wasn't yelling; I was too raw, the feelings too close to the surface. This was why I'd been avoiding him since the divorce. I didn't want his excuses, because I knew they wouldn't be good enough and I'd only feel more pain.

"Of course I loved you, and shit, Lila, I respected you and what you did for our family. It wasn't about you, it was about me not feeling like I meant anything to you. I went to the bar to meet the guys that night, but Joel called and canceled at the last minute, so I sat down and had a drink. I wasn't there looking for anything, I was just having as drink before coming home, when I felt a hand on my shoulder and Shirley Finkle sat down next to me. It was obvious she'd been drinking and I told you how she'd always had a crush on me in high school … She was looking at me in a way no one had looked at me in years. Like she *wanted* me. *Me.* She started saying stuff in my ear, telling me what she wanted to do to me and what she wanted me to do to her…"

"I don't need to hear the details," I said, my voice practically a whisper, as a pain I thought I'd beaten back bloomed within me.

"I don't know how we ended up in the Starbucks parking lot, all I know is that what she said and what she did drove me out of my mind. It felt good to be desired. I didn't intend for anything to happen, but it did and I've regretted it every second since."

I turned my head, unable to look at him any longer and noticed my perp grabbing her purse and waving to the other tellers. Shit, I needed to move. Which was actually perfect, because I wanted to get as far away from here as possible.

I put my hands up and pushed roughly against *The Douche's* chest, causing him to step back a few feet.

"Thanks," I said nastily, pushing past him toward the door. "Thanks for proving I made the right decision when I got rid of your ass. You're not the man I thought I'd married, you're just a weak shell of that man."

I gave him one last glance, ignoring the flash of hurt which was nothing compared to the gut-wrenching pain his words had inflicted on me and walked out after my perp.

I hoped she was guilty, because I was itching to nail someone's ass to the wall.

# Chapter 7

I was disappointed when I followed the young brunette into an upscale bistro on the other side of town. It was a happening lunch spot for local business people, a lot of whom were bank customers.

I figured she was *actually* stopping in for lunch but decided I'd stick with her just in case.

I got a table outside and ordered a wrap. I could see the perp inside from my vantage point *and* get some food in me at the same time. Two birds, one stone.

At first I didn't notice anything out of the ordinary. She seemed to know just about everyone in the bistro, probably a side effect of her job as a teller at the largest bank in town. She flitted from table to table as she waited for her order to be ready.

It was at the second table that I realized what she was doing. She threw her head back and laughed at something the older gentleman she was talking to had said and while his eyes roamed down to her quivering cleavage, she slid his pinky ring right off of his hand.

I don't know how he didn't feel it, although in his defense, she had a really great rack.

I paid close attention as she hopped around the dining room, taking a watch, a wallet, another ring, and a pocket watch. When I saw her take a pretty diamond hair clip out of a woman's hair, I had to admit, I was kind of impressed. I'd never seen slight of hand up close like that before and it took a special finesse to do what she did without getting caught.

Except, of course, she was getting caught ... on camera, by me ... but still it was impressive.

The perp sat and ate her meal as if she hadn't just robbed the entire clientele of the bistro, then said her goodbyes after paying her bill and left, just as carefree as when she entered.

I left money to cover my tab on the table and followed her a couple blocks down and a street over, to the local pawn shop.

I waited outside until I saw her walk up to the shop owner, talk for a minute, then follow him into the back room. Reaching my hand up to the top of the door, I opened it slowly, wrapping my hand around the bell before it could signal my entrance, then I eased inside.

Tiptoeing and keeping my breath even and as quiet as possible, I moved toward the back until I could hear their voices, then paused.

"Here's your take from last week," the man's voice said. "The old man with the Rolex actually thinks it's his son that stole it from him. I told him that I couldn't remember who I'd bought it from, but he's convinced. Said it was the final straw, he was cutting the boy off."

They both laughed and I felt a chill run through me.

They were running a con on the residents of the town. She stole their items and he sold them back to the victims, or probably anyone who came in and wanted to buy them, claiming someone sold them to him. Then they split the money from the sale.

*What dirty bastards…*

I left the shop as quietly as I'd entered it, going around the corner to the coffee shop to give her a chance to leave.

I went through the pictures I'd taken, then zoomed in on the pinky ring. It was sterling silver with a B engraved in it, and looked like it was very expensive. Although, I wasn't an expert on jewelry, so what did I know.

I enjoyed my latte, played a mindless game on my phone, then dropped my camera in the van before going back inside the pawn shop.

Plastering a big smile on my face, I sashayed into the store, the bell dinging as I entered.

"Afternoon," the man behind the counter said, and I turned my smile to him.

"Good afternoon, how are you on this fine day?" I asked, maybe a little too over the top.

"Better now," the man replied, his grin kind of lecherous.

Tapping down the desire to throw up in my mouth, I leaned over on the glass counter in front of him, treating him to a gratuitous shot of my cleavage. He took the bait, getting an eyeful before bringing his gaze back up to my face.

"What can I do for you, beautiful?"

The will to roll my eyes was great, but I controlled it, instead answering coyly, "Well, I don't know if you can help me or not … it's kind of a long shot… but I figured if anyone in this town would have what I need, it'd be you."

He smirked, obviously enjoying the attention and covered my hand with one of his.

"How about you tell me what you're looking for, and I'll see what I can do."

I stood up, pushed out my chest, and twirled a lock of hair around my finger.

"See, it's my daddy's birthday this weekend and I wanted to get him something *real* special. He's always worked so hard and could never afford the things he wanted ... He's always been a big fan of those mobster movies, really liked the jewelry the men wear and stuff, so I thought maybe if I could find a ring or a pendant or something, he'd get a kick out of it. His name's William, but he goes by Bill, so something with a W or a B would be just perfect."

I pouted in what I hoped was a pretty way, puffing out my lower lip and looking up at him from beneath my eyelashes.

"I told you it's a long shot..." I added, letting my sentence trail off as I ran a finger over my lower lip.

His eyebrows drew together and I worried maybe I'd laid it on a little too thick and he was on to me, when he held up a finger and said, "Just give me a minute," then disappeared into the back.

I watched him go then wandered over to the jewelry counter and leaned over looking inside. If he was monitoring me from the back, I wanted him to think I was searching for a piece for my father.

A delicate emerald ring had actually caught my eye when I heard him coming back to the front. Tearing my eyes away from the pretty piece of jewelry, I flashed my teeth at him as he stopped in front of me.

I watched as he laid out a chain, which had a large oval pendant with a big W engraved on it. When he didn't immediately put out anything else, I worried that he wasn't going to show me the ring, then he said, "I have this necklace and I also have a ring that you might like, but it's a bit more expensive."

He took my hand and turned it palm up, then dropped the pinkie ring inside.

I made a show of picking it up, looking it over, and placing it on my own pinkie and holding my hand up to look at it.

"Oh, it's perfect," I said, smiling up at him as if he were my hero. "How much is a *bit more expensive?*" I asked, keeping my tone cautious.

"Three hundred."

*Son of a bitch* ... I sure hoped Moose would pay me back for this.

"I'll take it," I replied, reaching for my purse. "My daddy's always given me the best presents, now I want to give back."

He smiled and rang me up, then placed the ring in a small box and handed it to me.

Before I could take the box, he grabbed my hand and asked, "How about dinner?"

I bit back a gag and replied sorrowfully, "Oh, I don't think my boyfriend would like that too much."

His face darkened, but before he could say anything, I yanked my hand out of his hand and said happily, "Thanks so much. Daddy's going to love it."

Then I got the hell out of there.

# Chapter 8

I felt like I was going to throw up.

*The Douche* had picked up the kids an hour earlier, not saying a word to me, probably still butt hurt over yesterday's exchange. I was curious over what *he* had to be upset about. I was the one who'd been told that all it took to get my husband to cheat on me was a stiff drink and some dirty talk.

As soon as I'd kissed my kids goodbye, I rushed to the shower and began the process of getting ready for my first date in over thirteen years.

I knew we were going to dinner, but I wasn't sure where, so I went with a short-sleeved, cobalt-blue jersey dress that matched my eyes perfectly and would be appropriate whether the restaurant was casual or fancy.

I used light makeup, just enough to highlight my features, and styled my hair in long, loose curls. I'd thought about straightening it, but ran out of time shaving every hair known to man off of my body.

*This took long enough to be embarrassing.*

Now I was ready. Heels on, clutch in my hand and waiting nervously for Cade to arrive.

I heard footsteps falling on the outside stairs and had to concentrate on my breathing so I wouldn't hyperventilate.

I bit back a squeak when the pounding started on the door and looked out the peephole.

*Holy shit*, he looked good.

I took in as much of him as I could through the tiny circular window. Motorcycle boots, dark jeans, and a red and black button-up shirt. His hair was down and I could see it had some curl to it, the dark tresses kept back off his face and falling to his shoulders and his beard looked groomed.

When he knocked again, I realized I'd been staring through the peephole long enough for him to get impatient, so I stepped back, took a deep breath, and opened the door.

His gaze started at my feet and slowly worked its way up, so by the time his eyes met mine, I felt like I'd just been given a full-body caress.

*Jesus!*

"Hi," I said, my voice coming out a little breathless from his perusal.

"You look gorgeous," was his reply, which caused me to grin broadly.

"Thanks, so do you."

"You ready?"

"Yeah." Then I looked down at myself and asked, "Will this be okay for the bike? I wasn't sure, but I didn't want to wear pants…"

Cade gave me a half grin and shook his head. "No, I wanna keep you safe, so that precious skin needs to be covered whenever you're on my bike," he said, pointing down at my bare legs.

"Oh, I thought … since you said you wanted me on your bike, that meant…" I stopped talking at his knowing grin and realized I'd just repeated what he'd said *verbatim*. Great, now he probably guessed I'd been replaying that little scene over and over in my head.

"I just meant I wanted you with me," he corrected, causing a nice tingle to run through me. "And you don't have to worry about it. I figured you'd dress up, so I brought my truck."

"Oh, okay," I said, pleased by his thoughtfulness, then stepped out and locked the door behind me.

As he pulled away I found myself looking at his large hands on the wheel. He was a big dude, probably somewhere around six foot three or four. Everything I'd seen about him so far had been large. His hands, his feet, his biceps. It made a girl wonder…

"What are you thinking about?" Cade asked with a deep chuckle, startling me out of my perusal and making my cheeks turn red.

"Um, I was just wondering where we're going," I lied through my teeth.

Rather than calling me on it he replied, "That Italian joint on Sixth."

"Mmmm, I love that place."

"Good."

I took in his jeans and button up, thought about it for a minute, then said softly, "Although, I think they require a jacket and tie."

Cade just smirked as he looked out at the road and said, "Don't worry about it, darlin'."

I decided to take his advice and not worry. I was going to be the new and improved Delilah Horton. Who dated hot, burly men and lived life without being so damn cautious.

When we arrived at the restaurant, Cade put his hand at the small of my back as he ushered me inside, which I had to admit, I really liked. I also noticed that every female from ages five to seventy noticed us walk in and had their eyes glued to Cade. This, I wasn't so sure I liked…

"Two for Wilkes," Cade said when the hostess asked how she could help. When she immediately led us back to our table, proving Cade was correct and something as insignificant as a *dress code* wasn't going to keep him out.

Thinking I just may be out on a date with the coolest guy I'd ever met, I smiled to myself as I picked up the menu and looked it over.

"What's the smile?" Cade asked.

I looked over my menu at him and replied honestly, "I'm just happy to be here … with you."

That earned me a sexy grin.

"Good," he replied, as the waiter stopped to get our drink order.

Guinness for me. Whiskey for Cade.

"I would have guessed you for a wine drinker."

"I like wine," I replied with a shrug. "But sometimes it goes to my head. With Guinness, I can keep my wits, while still enjoying a good drink."

"You don't want anything going to your head?" *God, it should be a sin to look as delicious as he did.*

"I think you're potent enough," I admitted with a laugh. "Since this is the first date I've been on in over thirteen years, I don't want to get bombed and embarrass myself."

"Thirteen years?"

"Yeah, my last date was with my husband before we got married."

"When'd you get divorced?"

"Ten months ago."

"And there's been no one since?"

"No. And honestly, we hadn't been with each other," I cleared my throat and continued softly, "*Intimately…* for a few years prior to the divorce. I guess I was upset, then bitter, and now, well, I haven't received any offers I was interested in … until yours."

I felt his hand hit my bare knee under the table and give it a little squeeze, which made me wonder, *how freakin' long are his arms?*

"Well, if it makes you feel better, this is the first date I've *ever* been on."

If I'd had something in my hand, I would have dropped it. As it was, I felt my jaw hit the floor as I asked, "Say what?"

"I'm not the kind of man who plans picnics and sends flowers," he said, squeezing my knee once more. "I've never taken a woman to the movies or out to dinner, unless it was my mom or sister."

"How's that possible?" I asked, not meaning to be rude, but honestly wondering how a man like him had never been in a relationship.

"Honestly," he said, eyes on me, face totally serious, "I've spent my adult life focused on other things. There've been women, all of them willing. They knew the score. It was just about fucking…"

I bit back a flinch at his brutal honesty, not really knowing how to respond.

"*Oh,*" was what I came up with.

"Yeah, *oh,*" Cade said, his smile softening his face, then gestured between us. "This is different for me, so it's kind of good that you're out of practice. Maybe you won't realize right away when I fuck up."

That made me laugh, then I asked, bewildered, "But why? I'm just a thirty-five-year-old single mom, who lives in a shitty apartment and takes pictures of people doing shit they're not supposed to."

"And that all works for you," he said, leaning forward, then sitting back when the waiter served our drinks and asked for our order.

Once he walked away, assuring us that our order would be

up soon, I took a sip of my perfectly chilled beer, then focused back on Cade.

I was a little freaked that he'd chosen me for his maiden voyage into dating. It was flattering, a little scary, and, frankly, a huge turn-on. Although the fact that he'd previous only been with women for *fucking* wigged me out.

He'd probably be a master at it and not only had I not had much practice, but one dirty talk from Slutty Shirley Finkle had been enough for my husband of twelve years to jump ship. I was terrified I'd be a disappointment if Cade and I ever got to that point.

"So, what exactly happened?" Cade asked, thankfully changing the subject.

"With what?"

"With your ex … and how'd you end up working for a PI?"

I settled back and said, "Well, they kind of go hand in hand. See, I found my husband cheating on me and even though my kids were in the car and I was beyond shocked, I had the fore-thought to snap a picture with my phone before I left him and immediately filed for divorce." I cleared my throat and hoped he didn't think I was a psycho, before going on. "Then, in a fit of rage and humiliation, I printed up copies of the picture and posted them all over town. Moose happened to see one and found out it was me who took it and why, then he offered me a job."

I looked up to see if he looked completely disgusted, and was surprised to see him grinning over his glass of whiskey.

"I think I saw that … Was it the beaver shot with the dude that looked like he was about to be murdered?"

"Yup, unfortunately, that was my ex … and yeah, she was pretty hairy."

"Looked like a fuckin' angry hedgehog."

I almost spit out my beer, but luckily got it down before I started laughing out loud.

"Yeah, it really did," I agreed.

The food arrived and I stopped laughing long enough to place some of their famous mouth-watering gnocchi in my mouth.

When Cade leaned across the table and said, "Your ex sounds like a total pussy," I had to agree.

"Yeah, he is … but I have to admit, it wasn't all him."

"How's that?" he asked, taking a big bite of lasagna.

"We could both tell there was something wrong for years and neither of us did anything to fix it. If it was that easy to get him to cheat, I obviously wasn't doing what I needed to do to keep him at home."

"I find that hard to believe."

"No really. I got caught up with the kids and being a mom and I didn't focus as much on him … on us. I wasn't the same then as I am now. I was a stay-at-home mom. I kept the house clean, put food on the table and helped the kids with home-work. I was a shadow of myself, but I didn't notice until it was too late."

"I don't think it's too late, I think it's right on time. That guy didn't know how to handle you, so you're better off. Anyone who would let a woman like you go, for a piece of snatch in the back of a beamer, is a jackass who doesn't *deserve* a woman like you."

"For someone who's never been on a date before, you sure are good at making me feel better about myself."

Cade just smiled and asked, "How's your food?"

"So good," I gushed. "Yours?"

"Best I've ever tasted," he said, and the look on his face made it seem like he thought the company had something to do with it.

On the drive home I began to get nervous again. A guy who fucked instead of dated probably didn't have any sort of three-date rule. What if he expected to come upstairs and get it on right away?

I wasn't sure I was ready for that, but at the same time, I didn't think I'd turn him away if he wanted to come in.

When he pulled in front of my apartment complex, I unbuckled my seatbelt so I could turn to him and ask, "Would you like to come inside?"

"Not tonight," he said, and the fear I'd been feeling quickly turned to disappointment.

"I feel like we talked about me all night. I didn't really get to learn anything about you."

"Next time," Cade said then reached over and pulled me across the bench seat so I was sitting flush against him. "If things go good between us, I'll give you all of it, but for now let's keep things about you."

My breath was coming in shallow pants at his nearness, the heat of his body seeping into mine, and it only got worse when he continued talking.

"We'll have dinner, coffee, go to the movies, whatever. And eventually I'll get my fists in all of this thick red hair." His hand slid up my back, into my hair, cupping the back of my head. "And I'll get to see those blue eyes go heavy with desire as I move above you." I felt my eyes getting heavy, just as he'd described and my lips parted as I tried to remain focused. "Seeing that lush ass move as you walk down the street, full of attitude and fire, the way your face lights up when you're laughing with your kids, and the way you felt, arms around my waist, tits against my back when I had you on my bike … Those are just some of the reasons I just became a man who dates."

I struggled for breath and asked without thinking, "What are you doing to me?"

"A woman like you should be confident in her sexuality, not

wondering where she stands, so I want you to know what I think about when I see you."

"Mmmmm," was all I managed, his dark eyes holding me hostage, then his gaze hit my lips and my tongue dashed out to wet them briefly.

That was the last thing I saw before I had the ability to do nothing but feel.

The combination of his soft lips and rasp of his beard sent waves of lust rolling through me upon contact. My mouth was already open and he needed no invitation; he was there, claiming me as his own and I was all too willing to submit.

I wanted to crawl into his lap, but I settled for shoving my hands in his curls and enjoying the soft feel against my fingertips. His hand was still at the back of my head, holding me in place as he tilted his head and deepened the kiss. I felt a liquid fire in my belly as his tongue swept through my mouth and I felt the whimper crawl up the back of my throat, not the least bit embarrassed when I emitted the sound.

If he wanted to be open and honest about the things he wanted to do to me, then he deserved to know I'd gladly strip down and offer myself up like a buffet to him right now in the cab of his truck.

When he pulled back I bit back the urge to protest, instead bringing my hand to my lips, as if wanting to hold his kiss there.

"I'll see ya," Cade said, and his words would have caused worry if I didn't see the massive bulge in his jeans, confirming he wanted me just as much as I wanted him.

"See ya," I said, then I opened the door and fell out of the damn truck.

# Chapter 9

I'd had a couple of days to get over my embarrassing exit from Cade's truck and now I was back to business as usual.

I hadn't heard from him but I wasn't worried. I decided to take him at face value and trust him when he said he's into me. That being said, I realized we weren't going to have a typical relationship, so I wasn't going to get worked up even though I hadn't talked to him in a few days.

We both had lives and I was sure when he had time, he'd get in touch.

I'd been wrapped up in a cocoon in my bed when I realized I didn't know how to get ahold of Cade. I didn't have his number, know where he lived or where he worked, so the ball was very much in his court.

My kids were safely back in school after a weekend RVing with their dad and although Elin had fun, Elena said if she never went camping in that thing again it would be too soon.

On my way out of Amy May's this morning, steaming cup of java in my hand, I'd stopped in the middle of the street when I heard someone calling my name. I turned to see Bea running after me, her uniform pressed and clean.

"Morning, Bea," I hailed as I walked back to the sidewalk to meet her.

"Hey, Lila, I was hoping to catch up," she said, not out of breath in the slightest.

*Maybe I needed to work out with her...*

"What's up?" I asked. "Why didn't you just shoot me a text."

"Cause I wanted to talk to you in person," she said, looking up at me. Bea was one of the few people I knew who made me feel like a giant.

"Shoot," I said, bringing my coffee cup to my lips to blow on it before taking a sip.

"Did I see you in Cade Wilkes' truck the other night?"

"There are ten thousand people in this town and you know whose truck I was in?"

"Just answer the question."

"Yeah, why?"

"Did you know he's part of an MC club a couple counties over?"

"An MC club?" I asked, my brain focusing on that rather than on what she was implying. "Doesn't MC stand for Motorcycle Club?"

Bea looked at me for a moment, then said, "I thought that the M and C came from motorcycle."

"I don't think so," I replied. "I think the C is for Club, so you just called it the Motorcycle Club Club."

Bea threw her hands up and asked, "Can you please be serious and answer the question?"

"No, I didn't know that ... How do you?"

"I make it a point to know who's living in my town, especially if they're part of an MC club ... or MC ... Whatever, you know what I mean."

"Isn't that like, racial profiling or something?"

I could tell she was getting exasperated with me, because it looked like her head was about to pop off. I could practically see steam.

"No it wouldn't be *racial* profiling, for God's sake, an MC isn't a race…"

"But it is *some* sort of profiling. You're keeping tabs on him because of what he does … who he is, not because he's actually done anything wrong. Am I right?"

Bea crossed her arms and glared at me.

"No, in the two years since he's been here, his life in the MC hasn't touched Greenswood or The Heights, but he's still an active member Lila. All I'm saying is that you need to know who you're going out with."

"Look, as my friend I appreciate you looking out for me. But, Bea, give the guy a break. If he's not doing anything illegal you shouldn't be warning people off of him."

I could tell she didn't like my response to her news, but I knew Bea and I knew she'd get over it. Still, it did give me a piece to the puzzle that was Cade. And now that she'd said it, being in an MC seemed like an obvious thing, given the little I knew about him.

I was in the library checking in when Moose contacted me and said he needed more dirt on the cokehead for his client. So I was currently following her large-breasted, platinum-blonde self into the Chinese place next to the sport's bar.

She was seated at a large round table toward the back of the restaurant with six other women. They were all around my age, but had more of a *trophy wife* look about them. Fake boobs, big lips, big hair and expensive clothes.

I walked through the dining area, skirting around their table to get to the sushi bar in the back. I picked the stool closest to them and ordered a hot tea, then opened my ears wide to eavesdrop.

"Oh my God," one of the blondes was saying. "Did you hear Cade Wilkes had a date the other night?"

*What the fuck?*

"No shit?"

"*No shit* ... I guess he's finally ready to do more than fuck and duck."

"Hmmmm, I wouldn't mind getting a shot at that..."

"*Mary!*"

"What? What Bob doesn't know won't hurt him."

This caused all the women to start laughing like hyenas while I sat there thinking Cade was right. When I didn't know who he was, I didn't hear anything about him, but now that he was on my radar it seemed like he was popping up all over the place.

How did everyone else in this town know who he was? Was I that oblivious to the world around me?

"All right ladies enough girl talk. I've got the stuff we've been talking about and Hector is ready to move forward."

I opened my compact mirror and looked behind me.

Just as I'd thought, the cokehead was the one who was talking, which made me wonder what kind of stuff she was talking about ... coke? And was she selling it to them or was something else going on?

I didn't think she'd pull out a bag of cocaine in the middle of the Chinese restaurant, but I still pulled out my cellphone and pretended I was taking a selfie, getting a shot of their table instead.

"Will it be just coke?" someone asked quietly behind me, and I swear my eyes were bugging out of my head.

*Are they seriously talking about that shit out loud in the middle of a restaurant? What kind of dumb fucks are they?*

"We can get coke, meth, crank, crack, roofies, or even that Devil's Breath..."

"Devil's Breath, what the hell is that?"

I leaned closer on my stool. I wanted to know what the hell Devil's Breath was myself.

"That's that new zombie shit. You blow it in someone's face, or have them smell it and it fucks them up for like … hours."

"*Shit,*" someone muttered and I totally agreed.

"Yeah, well, anyway, Hector can get just about anything we need. I just need you girls to get buyers, then let me know what and how much and I'll get you the shit. We get a ten percent cut off the top."

Holy shit, were these bitches going to be drug dealers? In our town?

I slipped off my stool and walked in the back as if I were going to the bathroom, then slipped out the back door.

"*Are you fucking kidding me?*"

My head swung up and I noticed the Camaro first, then the sleazy guy, who must be Hector standing next to it.

I was having the shittiest luck with these two.

Before he could say anything else, I was gone. Off like a shot, I ran around the corner and down the alley, my eyes looking everywhere for a place to hide. When I saw what I thought looked like Cade's bike, I dashed toward the sport's bar and ducked inside, hoping like hell Hector hadn't followed me.

I saw Cade sitting in the corner by himself, eating a sandwich, his eyes on the TV.

When I slid into the booth across from him, he took one look at my face and asked, "What the fuck?"

"That guy," I stuttered quickly, trying to get the words out. "The one from the day you picked me up, I just saw him again behind the Chinese place next door … And he saw me."

"Wait here," Cade said.

Then he was gone.

# Chapter 10

"Are you eating my fries?" Cade asked when he returned to his seat across from me.

I looked down at the fries in my fist and realized, *yeah, I was*, and I'd almost eaten them all.

"I need a cupcake," was my reply.

"Eddie," Cade called across the nearly empty room. "You have cupcakes?"

"Nah, but I have a chocolate lava cake."

I nodded eagerly when Cade looked to me for confirmation.

"That'll do," he yelled back.

"Coming right up."

"Did you see him?" I asked when he turned his attention back to me.

Cade shook his head and said, "No, just a Camaro peeling down the alley."

"I think that's his... I saw it both times."

"What'd you find this time?"

I leaned across the table and looked around to make sure

no one was close before whispering, "Hector, the sleazy guy with the Camaro is using the cokehead to rally the rest of the Country Club set. They're going to sell drugs in town to … I don't know, whoever will buy it, I guess, then report back to Hector and he'll supply it. The Coke Club is getting a ten percent cut off the top."

"You've gotta be shitting me."

"No, *no shit*," I replied, then sat back. "I gotta call my friend, Bea … She's a cop."

Cade's dark eyes came to mine.

"You're friends with a cop?"

"Yeah, she actually came to see me this morning, wanting to warn me off you."

I watched his back stiffen and wondered if I'd done the right thing, then I remembered I wanted to keep everything above board and be honest, so I wasn't going to let my fear of his reaction hold anything back.

"She did," he said, as more of a statement than a question, but didn't say anything else.

"Yeah, she thinks since you're part of an MC a few counties over, you may be dangerous and therefore *bad* for me…"

"And what do you think?"

Rather than answering right away, I kept right on with the honesty.

"And the Coke Club, they were talking about you too." When he just arched a brow in response I continued, "I guess you're the talk of the town because everyone saw you with a woman in your truck for the first time. The Coke Club is wondering if you're done with the *fuck and duck*…"

I didn't even wait until the bartender finished placing the lava cake in front of me before I dug in. I was already freaked out and the angry vibes coming off of Cade weren't helping anything.

"*Fuck and duck?*"

"That's what they said," I said around a mouthful of cake. "I've never heard that expression before, but I'm guessing it's because, like you said, you don't do relationships. A cruder way to say love 'em and leave 'em."

Cade folded his hands in front of him on the table and asked, "So are you asking if the stuff you heard today is true?"

I shrugged one shoulder and said, "Yeah, I guess, if you wanna tell me. I have to say, with all the drug stuff and hearing about that Devil's Breath, I haven't thought too much about the gossip."

That earned me a smile and I could see something flicker across Cade's face, like he'd just made a decision.

"I've been part of the MC for twenty years," he began as I continued to shovel chocolate in my cake hole. But I kept my eyes on him, so he'd know he had my attention. "They're my brothers, my family, and it's been my life longer than not. I've had my share of parties and pussy." I flinched internally, wondering if I'd ever get used to the blunt way he spoke. "But you can only do that shit for so long, so about two years ago I moved out here. Close enough to be there when they need me, but far enough away to have a life outside of the club."

I nodded to let him know I was still with him and because what he said made sense.

"And the Coke Club had their panties in a twist because although I fuck, I don't fuck in the neighborhood pool, so to speak."

*I don't think that's the way that expression goes,* I thought, then scooped up my last bite of chocolaty goodness.

"I've never been with anyone in this town," he said.

"Until me," I whispered, then lowered my eyes, the look in his too intense for me to take at that moment.

I began studying the rings on his hands, suddenly fascinated by the chunks of silver adorning his fingers.

"Until you," Cade agreed softly, then brought one of those

51

big hands to my chin and tilted my face back up to him. "What happens at the club won't touch you. If things get serious and we start playing meet the family, I'll take you to a barbecue or a dinner and introduce you to the guys and their old ladies, but that's it. I don't want *my* woman hanging out at the clubhouse or taking to those bitches who hang around the compound looking for a good time. Your kids will never see it and that life will never touch your life. You got it?"

"Yeah," I replied softly.

"I won't always tell you what goes down when I'm at work. I'm a guy who gets stuff done and not all that stuff is good, but like I said … it won't touch you."

"Okay."

"And while we're talking, I'll say this. I already told you that I'm not a man who does flowers, but you gotta know, I'm also not the type of man who settles down and has a white picket fence."

"I don't need that," I replied honestly. "I had it once and it didn't take."

Cade gave me a slight nod and ran his thumb along my lower lip.

"What about a chain-linked fence and a cat?" I asked, needing to lighten the mood.

"*Fuck no*," he said with a scowl. "I hate cats."

"Why?" I asked. "They're low maintenance and have personality."

"They shit in the house and stare at you with their freaky-ass eyes. No way, no cats."

I laughed and he smiled along with me.

"Thanks," I said, reaching my hand out to his free one and giving it a squeeze.

"For what?"

"For being here, for running after sleazy Hector and for being honest with me."

"You can count on that," he promised, and I really hoped he was telling the truth.

# Chapter 11

"Hey, Elin, how about you help me man the grill?"

I looked over from my perch at the counter in Amy May's kitchen and mouthed, *thank you*, to her husband Jason. I watched with a smile as Elin put down his tablet and went out to help Jason make dinner. The girls, Elena and Amy May's daughter, Cassidy, were in Cassidy's room doing Lord knows what while Amy May and I were in the kitchen, drinking wine and catching up.

When the guys went outside, Amy May put the knife down on the cutting board and leaned closer to me.

"So what you were saying earlier..." she whispered. "Do you think that's true, about the Country Club wives selling drugs?"

"That's what it sounded like and that's what I told Bea. She hasn't heard of this Hector before, but she said she'd talk to some of the other cops ... have them get with their informants."

"What did Moose say?"

"He said the shot of all the women was good, but he needs more. He needs to see an actual hand off."

"Don't you think that's kind of dangerous?"

"Yeah, of course, but Bea and the cops are looking into it and Cade knows about him. He said he'd see what he can find out."

"You need to be careful. That Hector guy has seen you, twice … Maybe you should tell Moose to get his own shots for this one."

I shook my head and insisted, "I'll be fine. This client is paying big bucks and my cut is the largest one I've seen."

"It's not worth it if it's dangerous. Does Moose know you talked to the cops, and Cade, about the case?"

"No, I think he'd be pissed if he knew, but what am I supposed to do? He may not have a problem dealing with criminals and offering up proof of illegal activities, but I do. I wouldn't feel right keeping something like this to myself."

"No, you're right, and I totally agree with you about not keeping it to yourself; now I just wish you'd back off … But, I know you and know you won't."

"We can't have people dealing drugs in town and really, this Hector guy is smart, picking rich white women to do his dirty work. No one would think to even suspect. I know I wouldn't."

"Do you know who Moose's client is?"

"No and I don't know if I want to. Really, the less I know the better. I just want to know I had a hand in bringing Hector and the Coke Club down … To feel like I did something good for this town."

"You always do, babe," Amy May said, then her eyes went to the door and she stopped talking.

I took a drink of wine and asked, "Do we have dessert?" as Jason and Elin walked inside with a platter of hamburgers and hot dogs.

"Is my name Amy May?" she asked with a grin, which I answered with one of my own, knowing there were cupcakes in my future.

Later that night when the kids were getting ready for bed, I was sitting in the living room, my comfy pajamas already on, and getting ready to watch an old episode of *Friends*, when Elena came in and sat next to me.

When she didn't immediately start talking, I put down the remote and asked, "What's up, baby girl?"

"Um, I was just wondering," she began, twirling her hair around her finger in what I knew was a nervous gesture. "Are you happy?"

"Yeah, baby, of course," I assured her, my hand going to her shoulder. "Why do you ask?"

"Well, when we got back to Dad's house after camping, there was someone waiting there. Dad said she's his girlfriend."

I schooled my features even as my stomach clenched and replied, "Elena, your dad and I have been separated for almost a year now, it's normal for him to start dating again."

My precious girl bit her lip and looked at me with a worried expression.

"He said they've been together for a while, but he waited to introduce her, as his girlfriend, until they were serious."

"They're serious, huh?" I asked, not really wanting to know about *The Douche's* love life, but needing to for my children's sake.

"They're moving in together," she said softly.

*Oh, Hell no…*

Elena was watching me closely, as if she was worried this information was going to hurt me. It didn't, but it did piss me off. First he gets an RV to show off for the kids and now he's moving in some strange woman and introducing her to *our* kids without even talking to me about it?

This went against everything we'd discussed when we split.

We didn't agree on much, but we'd both said we wouldn't subject our children to random people unless we entered into a serious relationship. And if that happened, we were going to give the other person a head's up.

I guess that agreement flew out the fucking window, although what did I expect? If our vows didn't matter to him, why would a random promise.

Hoping I was successfully keeping all emotion off my face, I pulled my lips into the best smile I could manage and said, "Okay, baby girl, I'll talk to your dad about it. But I'm sure if he's serious enough to move in with her, she must be a nice person."

*Unless he was moving in with Slutty Shirley Finkle.*

It didn't even bear thinking and I was going to try and hold off on getting upset until I talked to him myself.

"Thanks for talking to me about it, Elena. You know I'm always here no matter what, okay?"

When she got up and started to leave the room, I added, "And you don't have to worry about me, okay? I'm happy."

As I watched my daughter walk away, that worried expression still on her face, I thought, *Damn, looks like I have to make another trip to the bank.*

# Chapter 12

"Who're you here to spy on this time?" *The Douche* asked as I entered his office, not even bothering to rise from his desk.

"What?" I asked, confused not only by his question, but by his demeanor.

"C'mon, Delilah, give me a break … I know you think I'm an idiot, but do you really think I'm stupid enough not to know what you're doing?"

"What am I doing?" I asked, trying to give attitude to cover up the fact that he'd thrown me.

"Working with that PI, sneaking around and taking pictures of people to get them in trouble," he answered calmly, his hands together on his desktop.

"How do you know?" I asked, no longer playing coy.

"I've heard chatter. About people getting caught cheating and stuff, then I noticed you slinking around by a motel one day when I was driving home. But when you came in here the other day, *finally* ready to give me the opportunity to explain myself … Well, that confirmed it for me. I saw you run out as soon as Tracey left on her break."

I mentally kicked myself for not being a better actress, then felt the need to assure him, "The kids don't know. No one really does, at least, *I thought* no one did ... I guess I wasn't being as discreet as I thought."

"So, what are you doing? Working as a PI with that jackass Moose?"

"No, I'm an Investigative Photographer," I made that up off the top of my head, and really liked the way it sounded. "Moose does the PI work and deals with clients, I just take the pictures."

"Sounds like it could be dangerous."

"It's not, I swear," I assured him, then wondered why I was defending myself when I'd come there to confront him. "Anyway, that's not why I'm here."

"Oh? You aren't here to spy on Tracey again?"

I looked through the glass of his office at the woman who was back in her spot at the desk, then back at him.

"No, not today. I'm here because Elena had a talk with me last night. She wanted me to know that you introduced them to your girlfriend, who is, *apparently,* moving in with you."

*The Douche* crossed his arms over his chest, the defensive gesture he always went to whenever I brought up something he didn't want to discuss.

"*Okay...*" he muttered warily.

"I thought we agreed to talk about it before we introduced the kids to anyone *special* in our lives."

He sighed and admitted, "You're right, we did ... And I meant to talk to you about it. But then you came in last week and things didn't go so well and I never got around to it. I'd talked to Mary about pushing back our plans to tell the kids, but she's already put in notice on her rental, so we couldn't really do that?"

"Why didn't you call or shoot me a text ... *something?*" I argued, then what he'd said penetrated. "Mary?"

"Yeah, *Mary,*" he replied, his arm waving out toward the

office a few feet away, where Mary, one of the loan officers he'd worked with for the past ten years sat. "Didn't the kids say?"

I felt like I'd been punched in the gut.

*Mary?* Did that mean Slutty Shirley Finkle wasn't the one-time deal I'd thought? Had he cheated before? Had he been cheating on me for *years?* Mary'd been to our house. I'd invited her over for holidays and family gatherings, worried she'd be alone if I didn't … Had I been made a fool this whole time?

Some of what I was thinking must have been conveyed on my face, because *The Douche* held up his hands.

"No, no, *no. Lila,* it's not what you're thinking … Mary and I were never together before. We've only been seeing each other for six months."

"And you're already moving in together?" I asked, not ready to believe him.

He ran a hand over his face and looked over at Mary, who was watching us through the glass, a worried expression on her face.

I tried to ignore the fact we were on display and kept my attention on my ex-husband.

"It may seem like it happened quickly, but we've known each other for so long … *just as friends* … so the relationship felt like it started in the middle, you know? I swear, nothing ever happened before. Mary will vouch for that and you know she's a good woman."

He was right, I did know that, but still … I felt my eyes sliding over to look at her. Barely five foot two, carrying about one hundred and eighty pounds, and forever styling her hair in a bob, Mary had always been a friend. She was a mom-type person, always looking out for others. Calling if you were sick, making a casserole for work dinners, and always having a fresh batch of cookies in her cookie jar at home. She was probably a good five years older than me, and I'd always felt comfortable around her.

Now I didn't know what to think. She was the exact opposite of Slutty Shirley Finkle and not the kind of woman I envisioned *The Douche* going for once our divorce was final.

"Elena didn't say it was Mary?" he asked, pulling me out of my thoughts.

"No, she didn't," I replied, chewing on my lower lip as I tried to decide how I felt about this new information.

"I was planning to tell you, I promise, and I want you to know that if everything goes well with our living together, I plan to ask Mary to marry me."

*Holy shit. The hits just kept coming...*

I swung my gaze to him and asked, "Really?"

"Yes, Delilah. We have a good thing going and she needs me. That feels good."

I accepted that jab and turned to go, needing to get out of his office and away from all of the knowing eyes ... especially Mary's.

"Okay, well, I'm happy for you," I mumbled, almost truthfully, as I started out the door.

"Thanks," he called after me, then added, "And, Delilah, be careful out there, all right?"

I didn't turn, but just nodded and kept going.

I didn't stop until I reached Amy May's, heading right for the counter, sitting down, and yelling, "*Cupcake!*"

Ten seconds later a beautiful chocolate cupcake with Oreo frosting and chocolate shavings was set in front of me.

I dug in without even looking up.

*Heaven.*

# Chapter 13

I realized I hadn't had anything to eat all day except a cupcake, so I stopped by a hot dog vendor on the way to the motel. I was chowing down on my fully loaded dog when my cell pinged an incoming text.

I NEED **the pics from the Jones job ASAP. Then I have more info about the wareabouts of the druggies... I need more on them.**

UGH, *Moose.*

I wasn't sure that wareabouts was even a word, but I got the gist of what he was saying. I usually enjoyed my job – catching cheating bastards in the act gave me a little thrill – but this drug dealer stuff was starting to make me nervous. Hector seemed like bad news and I didn't like the fact that he'd seen my face ... twice.

Still, the payout on this job was twice what I normally

made, which meant I could get my kids some cool Christmas gifts.

*Oh, and pay my rent.*

I went to the address Moose had given me earlier in the day, watching for movement as I drove past it and parked my van a block away.

I hadn't seen anything, but that didn't mean the perps weren't inside. They were adulterers after all, so they wouldn't exactly be boning in the front yard.

I checked the neighborhood, which was quiet and void of people, before jogging around the back of the houses and creeping up to the one I was looking for. I peered in the first window, finding the kitchen empty, before crouching down and making my way awkwardly to the next one.

I rose slowly, taking in the bookshelf and desk, before movement by the door captured my attention.

The man was turned toward me, but his hands were lifted up, holding on to the door jamb, his head thrown backward. The last thing in the world he was going to do was look out the window and pay attention to me, so I felt safe drawing my eyes downward to see what was putting that horrifying look of pleasure on his chubby face.

The full view was nothing to write home about. He was totally naked, and really hairy in areas that were not pleasing to the eye. He had not only chest hair, but patches of hair on his stomach and a thick line leading down to his big, unruly bush.

*There was nothing happy about that trail...*

I almost tossed my cookies.

Knelt before him was a fully clothed brunette, her head bobbing back and forth as she went to town on his junk. With every movement, I caught glimpses of his penis. Red and angry, it was small enough for her to deep throat with no trouble.

*I'm never eating hot dogs again*, I thought as I raised my camera, took enough shots to get faces, position, nudity, and the room, before hightailing it out of there.

Seriously worried the loaded hot dog I'd eaten was about to make a repeat appearance, I braced my hands against the side of my van and hung my head. I breathed deeply in and out, letting the fresh air calm my stomach. Once I felt my food settle, I jumped and headed back to town.

I parallel parked in the library parking lot and called Moose, figuring it would be easier to let him know I was about to email him the shots and get the details of what he needed for the Coke Club case.

Once I was done with the computer, I waved goodbye to Claire and walked out of the library, punching out a text to Bea as I walked.

**CAN you and Shannon hang with my kiddos tonight for a few hours? I have to work. Thx.**

I WAS ALMOST to my car when the roar of pipes hit my ears, and I looked up to see Cade riding toward me. I tried to contain my excitement as I watched him draw near, but didn't bother trying to keep the happy smile from lighting up my face.

"Hey," he said while he idled beside me.

"Hi," I replied, my eyes devouring every inch of him. I don't know how it was possible, but he seemed to get hotter every time I saw him.

"Your kids gone this weekend?"

"Not Friday, but Saturday."

"I'll pick you up," he said. "Dinner at my place."

My heart jumped at the thought of seeing where he lived.

"Sounds great," I replied, not caring how eager I sounded. I totally was…

"Six," he said, then gave me a wink and drove away.

I watched him, breathless with anticipation, then looked down at my phone to see that Bea had replied. She and Shannon could be over at seven.

I texted back, **Perfect**, then looked up for one last glance of Cade's retreating form, before getting in my van and heading home.

I made sure my kids were fed, their homework was done and they were ready for school the next day, before Bea and Shannon came over. I wanted the evening to go as smoothly as possible for them. The kids loved them, so they'd probably want to hang out until bedtime, but at least I knew everything else was done.

You'd think that would ease some of my guilt at leaving them, but I always felt guilty leaving them with someone else when I had to work. That had never happened while I was married to *The Douche* and it was just one more thing I could admit I blamed him for … bitter shrew that I am.

After meeting Cade and actually talking to my ex and coming to terms with some of my issues, I was hoping that soon, I too would be happily moving on.

I was ready to let this anger and bitterness go. We'd been unhappy bedfellows for so long though, I was worried it would take more than a few good conversations for that to happen.

Maybe a great bout of sex with Cade would help things move along faster.

It was thoughts like that that were making me equal parts ecstatic and terrified about going to his house for dinner.

I left my apartment, knowing my kids were happily chatting Bea's ear off and turned my van toward a popular joint in The Heights, which was known for its tapas and killer cocktails. Moose said he'd heard word of a couple of the Coke Club women meeting Hector there tonight, so I was all dressed up in a cute tank top and mini-skirt, ready to blend in with the evening crowd.

The parking lot was full, so I valeted the van, smiling sweetly at the young stud who was eyeing my baby with disdain.

*Guys just didn't get the benefits of driving a minivan.*

I walked straight to the bar on thin heels, my hair fluffed out and full, my makeup a little heavier than I usually wore it, but this was Tapas in The Heights. You didn't show up looking like a scrub.

Like this, I blended. If I'd shown up in my regular uniform of jeans and a T-shirt, I would have stuck out like a sore thumb.

I'd just ordered a dirty martini from the bar, when I noticed one of the big-breasted blondes from the Chinese place walking into the back and entering the hallway that led to the restrooms.

I was about to follow, when familiar face caught my eye.

Tall and built, with short dark hair and glasses, Amy May's husband, Jason, was always easy to spot in a crowd. Seeing him was unexpected, so it took me a minute to realize it was him and he was *here*.

I started toward him, my hand raised to get his attention, when I saw him approach a woman at the other end of the bar.

I dropped my unseen hand slowly, taking in the scene before me.

Jason leaned down to whisper something in the raven-haired woman's ear. Whatever it was caused him to smile and I watched as he put his hand on her back and began rubbing in slow circles.

My stomach clenched painfully and my eyes watered, even

as I prayed I wasn't *really* seeing what I was seeing. Maybe I was having a mild stroke, which brought on visions...

Still, I instinctively pulled my phone out of my clutch and pressed the camera button.

I turned and brought the phone up, flipping the screen as I readied the camera for another fake selfie. When the camera came into focus and I snapped a shot of Jason leaning down to kiss the mystery woman, catching both of their profiles in the shot, I wasn't even aware of the tears running down my face.

The busty blonde and Hector forgotten, I left my still-full martini glass and fled the Tapas bar.

I cried all the way home, wondering how I was going to break the news to my best friend that her husband was a cheating bastard.

# Chapter 14

"I don't care if you had a heart attack and needed an ambulance, when I give you a job and tell you to get me pictures, I want you to get me those fucking pictures no matter what!"

I was holding my cell up to my ear, mouth open in shock, while Moose screamed his head off through the phone. I'd never heard Moose angry before, and he'd *never* talked to me like that before.

Of course, I'd never left a job without getting my shots, after seeing my best friend's husband with another woman before either.

I'd thought Moose would be upset, but understanding, when I told him I'd left the Tapas bar last night without getting the evidence he needed.

That was not the case.

"If you don't get your shit together and get me those shots today, I'll find someone else who can … and you can forget about me doubling your pay."

Moose hung up before I could even get a word in edgewise,

and I felt my already heavy heart fall even further into the pit of my stomach.

I didn't want to lose my job. And I didn't want to do what I was about to do either…

I took a deep breath and tried to keep the tears that had been flowing all night at bay, as I opened the door to Amy May's bakery and walked toward her office.

I knew she'd be in there, as she was every morning, looking over numbers, checking the schedule, and jotting down new recipe ideas. I fought the urge to turn tail and run, instead forcing myself to take each step closer to ruining Amy May's life.

I rapped on the door, and when Amy May called, "Come in," I entered her domain and gave her a shaky smile.

Amy May noticed my demeanor right off and swiveled in her chair.

"What's wrong?"

"Can I sit?" I asked, pointing helplessly to the chair next to her desk.

"Of course," she replied, giving me a once-over, as if to make sure I wasn't physically injured. "What's going on?"

I sat down, clutching my purse in my lap, my cell phone in my hand, and said, "Amy May, I have something to tell you…"

My heart lodged in my throat, causing me to pause.

"Are you sick? Is something wrong with the kids?" she asked, sensing it was something major.

"No," I assured her with a shake of my head. "It's nothing like that. It has to do with Jason."

Amy May's hand came to her heart and she asked, "Is he okay?"

"Yes, he's fine," I replied, letting go of my purse to reach my hand out and clasp hers. "I'm just going to say this quick … Rip the Band-Aid off, so to speak…"

She watched with wide eyes as I picked up my phone and found the picture I was looking for. I kept it toward me, then turned it and explained, "I saw Jason with another woman last night, at the Tapas bar in The Heights ... I'm so sorry, Amy May."

Amy May took the phone out of my hand and studied the picture, then her face turned red and her free hand covered her mouth.

I braced, ready for hysterics, then got the second shock of my life when rather than crying, she started to giggle.

"*Amy May,*" I said softly, thinking she was losing it.

She busted out in a full-on laugh after that, then shook her head and said, "Sorry, Lila, I didn't mean to laugh, especially when you look so devastated, but Jason isn't cheating on me."

"I was there last night," I replied, taking the phone and pushing it into her face. "Look at the picture, Amy May, the evidence is right in front of you."

"You look at the picture," she said, turning my hand so the camera was facing me. "Look at her face, Lila ... That's me."

"*What?*" I asked, squinting to look at the picture, then realized what I was doing and touched the screen to zoom in on the woman. It was hard to tell in profile, but I could see that the woman did resemble Amy May. "What are you talking about?"

Amy May blushed as she explained, "Well, you know what it's like, being married as long as Jason and I have ... Sometimes we like to spice things up and role play."

"*What?*" I asked again, this time shouting.

"It was just for fun. I get dressed up, put on a wig, and go to a bar. Then he shows up and we pretend to be strangers. He picks me up and we go to a hotel... "

I sat there, staring at her, eyes wide before I blinked one time slowly.

"You're telling me I spent the night in emotional hell, *devastated* that a man I love and trust was cheating on my best friend and it was all really just you guys playing out your kinky sex life?"

Another giggle, then Amy May replied, "Well, I don't know how *kinky* it is, but it does keep things interesting." She covered my hand with her own and said, "I'm sorry you were worried and I really do appreciate you looking out for me, but, honey, all men aren't like your ex. Jason wouldn't cheat on me."

I hung my head and said, "I know that, I do. I just saw you from behind and freaked out. I'm sorry ... *Don't tell Jason?*"

"Oh, I *have* to tell Jason," Amy May said with a laugh when I looked at her with despair. "He's gonna die!"

"He's going to hate me," I countered, worried he'd see it as a betrayal, since he was also my friend.

"You know better than that," she said, then took pity on me and added, "I made some cream puffs this morning. Want some?"

I nodded, knowing my face looked pitiful as I sulked about looking like a fool.

"Lila," Amy May said, pulling me up to stand with her. "I love you."

"Love you, too, Amy May."

# Chapter 15

After that embarrassing, but happy, turn of events with Amy May and Jason, I was happy to be hot on the trail of another perp.

I needed to go in, get the shots, and prove to myself I had what it took to do this job.

I needed a little reassurance.

So, I was back at the sleazy motel. This time on the second floor, following a lead Moose had sent about a man who was suspected of sleeping around.

Right in my wheelhouse...

I'd followed the man, a tall, distinguished-looking man who appeared totally out of place in this part of town, and a stringy-haired brunette with literally the biggest tits I'd ever seen in my life. No way those things were real. In fact, I figured she must have to special order bras and tops and stuff, because those things were impossible to contain.

I'd been getting ice out of the machine as part of my cover and almost got hit with a nipple when she walked past me.

I paid attention to what room they went in, but found luck was not with me when I saw they'd drawn the curtains.

Knowing I needed to prove myself to not just Moose, but to myself, I racked my brain for a solution. I needed these shots.

Coming to a conclusion, I reached my hand up and knocked loudly on their door, then took off running and hid around the corner.

"Who the hell is it?" I heard the man call out.

"Nobody's there," the woman replied, and I heard the door shut behind her.

I waited a few beats, then ran quickly on the balls of my feet so as not to make too much noise and knocked again, not stopping as I ran past their room and down the other way. I rounded the corner just as I heard the door open again.

"Are you fucking kidding me?" the woman whined in a nasally voice and I had to bite back a giggle.

"No one again?" the man asked, and I heard movement. "Fuck this shit."

Luck was with me this time, because when I peeked around the corner, I saw them both shuffling down the balcony away from where I was hiding. I wasn't sure if they'd gone all the way downstairs, or were just on the other side of the wall by the stairs, but I knew this was my only shot.

I sprinted as quietly as I could to their open door, dashed in, and eased the curtains open enough so that I could see in, but hopefully not so much they would notice.

I was about to run back out when I heard the clamoring of footsteps coming back to the room.

*Shit*, I screamed inside my head, then hurried across the room and into the bathroom, closing the door most of the way and praying no one had to go to the bathroom anytime soon.

I heard them coming back into the room, then the door shut behind them.

"Did you see anyone?" Nasally Voice asked.

"Nah, probably just some punk ass kids," the man growled.

"Now get back on the chair and unleash those sweet tits for me."

I thought I heard the woman sigh, but couldn't be sure from my position in the bathroom. I could see through the crack of the door and was able to focus my lens on the bed and see everything that was going on.

She sat back in the chair, took off her tank top, and unleashed her bodacious tatas. It seemed a little weird when the man crawled up into her lap and cradled his face in her breasts, but I figured he just had a big boob fetish and began snapping shots.

When he started suckling on her nipple, I guessed we were getting to the good stuff, but after a few minutes went by, they didn't move to the bed, and he kept sucking, I realized with a shutter of revulsion that he had some sort of mommy/baby fetish.

He was nursing.

She'd just been sitting there, bored while he suckled, then got called into the game when he reached for her hand and placed it on his throbbing dick.

I took a couple more pictures of him nursing and some of her jacking him off. Then the scene in front of me, paired with the weird moans coming from the man, had me backing away from the crack in the door to sit on the toilet, my hands over my ears.

If he started crying like a baby, I was out of there. I didn't care if I got caught or not.

Thankfully there were no baby noises, just the sound of the man coming and I hoped, since there was no actual sex, no one would have to come to the bathroom to clean up. Although, I was sure the woman would want a shower after what she'd just endured.

I waited for what felt like forever, but finally heard the man thank the woman, then the opening and shutting of the door.

My heart pounded as I listened to what sounded like the woman getting closer to the bathroom. I got behind the door just as it opened and listened to the sound of running water as the woman washed her hands.

When she left without shutting the door or needing to use the toilet, which was right in front of me, I closed my eyes and thanked my lucky stars.

I heard shuffling around and what sounded like her leaving, but I still gave it a few seconds before I exited the bathroom slowly and looked around. When I saw that I was *actually* alone, I let out the deep breath I'd been holding.

Peering out the door, I left the room when I saw the coast was clear and hurried downstairs. When I made it to the bottom, I was headed to my car, home free and relieved, when a familiar voice called to me and I stopped in my tracks.

Holding my stomach to try and contain the rolls of nausea and fright, I turned my head to give the man from upstairs a shaky smile.

"What was that?" I asked him, honestly not sure what he'd said.

"Did you see any kids running around?" he asked as he moved *way* too close to where I was standing. "My wife and I were trying to take a nap and someone kept knocking on our door."

I fought an eye roll at the wife comment and shook my head as his eyes wandered down my body. I fought the urge to shield my unimpressive bosom from his beady eyes, but realized that's not what he was looking at when he asked, "Are you okay?"

"Oh, yeah," I said, looking down to where my hand was clutching my stomach. "Just cramps."

I found that if you talked about cramping or periods in any given situation it almost always caused the other person to redirect and change the subject, or sometimes even walk away.

I was hoping for the latter in this case, instead *he* rolled *his* eyes and said, "I'm so tired of you women using that shit as an excuse. Any time you don't want to do anything you blame it on cramps and periods. Well, I call bullshit."

After what I'd just witnessed back in that room, the last thing I wanted was this man judging me, or any women for that matter, so what he said really pissed me off.

With my hands on my hips I yelled, "Oh, really? Bullshit? I'd like to see you bleed out of your dick for one week every month and see how you fucking deal!"

I didn't wait for him to reply, I just stomped off to my car, got in and drove off, leaving him staring after me with a scowl.

# Chapter 16

I'd managed to make it through the rest of my week without any other embarrassing assumptions. What I didn't do, however, was find hide or hair of any of the Coke Club or Hector. Suffice it to say, Moose was not happy with me, but if I didn't see anything, it was impossible for me to get a picture of it.

Now I was riding on the back of Cade's bike, snuggled happily against his back as we cruised out to his place. I was really excited to see where he lived. Curious about how he lived and totally planning to snoop as much as I could to learn more about him.

I'd taken the time to straighten my hair, which because of its thickness and curl took almost an entire hour to accomplish. Unsure of what the plan for the night was, I hadn't felt comfortable packing an overnight bag ... I didn't want to look presumptuous. But I did bring my big purse, which concealed my toothbrush, fresh underwear, and a rolled-up maxi dress, because who was I kidding, I totally hoped I was having a sleepover at Cade's!

The roar of the machine between my legs did nothing to

ease the ache I felt after what seemed like weeks of foreplay with this unbelievably virile man. If he didn't initiate something that night, I was afraid I'd totally embarrass myself by humping his leg.

That's how badly I needed to get off.

We drove out past The Heights, then down a long road with houses scattered a few acres apart. When we started to slow, I looked around Cade's massive body to see a beautiful log cabin home in the distance.

I immediately fell in love.

Beautiful stone pillars accented the front porch, which held a couple Adirondack chairs.

That was all I saw before he pulled the bike up next to his truck and turned it off. I retrieved my purse from the side satchel thingy, then followed him around the truck to the front of the house, my eyes taking in every inch of the beautiful wood features.

Cade opened the door and I had a second to wonder why it wasn't locked, when a large black beast darted out and headed straight for me.

Before I had a chance to register what was what, the large black lab's snout beelined right for my crotch. I tried unsuccessfully to push the dog's head back and when that didn't work, I maneuvered my body by turning my hips to the side.

Finally, Cade saved me by saying sternly, "Rufus," and the dog immediately left me to go sit next to his master.

I knew I'd turned red, it was always embarrassing when a dog sniffed your crotch, but it was even more so when you were with a scary hot guy who was grinning down at you.

I lowered my head, trying to compose myself, when Cade's heat hit me and his breath caressed my ear as he murmured, "If it were socially acceptable, I'd greet you in the same way."

*Okay, that just embarrassed me more*, even as it made the lust curl deep in my belly.

I reached up and slapped Cade on the arm without lifting my head and heard him chuckle as he walked away. I took a few deep breaths, told myself to move on and cover myself anytime Rufus came near, then followed Cade inside.

I shut the door behind me, swiveling my head back and forth, taking everything in as I entered his living space.

With an open floor plan, it looked like one large room, with a living room, kitchen, dining area, and a staircase in the back corner. The furnishings were manly and rustic, fitting the house beautifully. There were even some beautiful wood carvings Cade had made into a coffee table and dining room table.

"It's gorgeous," I breathed as I walked around circling his space.

Cade was leaning against his kitchen counter, absently petting Rufus as he watched me with a small smile.

"Thanks. I knew what I wanted, planned it out for years. When I was finally ready, I worked with a builder to create exactly what I'd envisioned. I'm happy with the way it turned out."

"I bet," I replied, then wandered over to look at the framed picture on his mantel. "Is this your family?"

The photograph showed Cade with who I assumed were his parents and sister. They all had the same glossy dark hair, tanned skin, and intense eyes. Cade was in the picture too, and they were all standing on a hilltop or mountain, overlooking the ocean and laughing.

They were a striking group.

"Yeah, that's my mom, pop, and younger sister, Alani."

"Is this Hawaii?"

Cade nodded, then pushed off the counter and moved toward me.

"That's where I'm from. My family is still there."

"What made you leave?" I asked, my chin lifting to hold his eyes as he came up next to me.

"I came to the mainland to go to school. Play ball. But things didn't work out with football, and I quickly realized without it, I didn't want to be in college. So, I got a job rebuilding motorcycles … That's how I met some of my brothers. I joined the club and the rest is history."

"Why didn't you go home when you left school?"

"I felt like a failure. An embarrassment to my father. I wanted to make something of myself on my own, not run back and ask for their help."

"Do you go back to visit?"

"At least once a year," he replied, then, obviously done talking about his family, he asked, "Are you hungry? I can start dinner."

"Can I see the rest of your house first?"

I honestly asked because I was really curious to see the upstairs, but thought maybe Cade thought I wanted to go upstairs for something else, because his eyes darkened and his lips curled up seductively.

*Yikes! I don't know if I'm ready,* I thought as I followed after him on shaky legs.

The upstairs was also one big room, like a loft, with the biggest bed I'd ever seen on one side, and the coolest shower ever built on the other. It was glass with large pieces of wood on the outside, and beautiful blocks of stone acting as the floor. There was a door off to the side, leading, I assumed to the rest of the bathroom, and large woven rugs spread throughout the space.

"That shower is amazing," I said as I walked closer to get a better look. He had benches lining the wall next to the shower, and hooks hanging for towels and clothes.

"We can test it out later, if you'd like," he murmured from next to me, causing me to jump. I hadn't heard him come up behind me. His nearness, paired with the meaning behind his words, had my body going up in flames.

I laughed nervously, choosing not to answer, then looked back at the beautiful bed. I glanced from the bed to the shower, becoming even more flustered when I realized that if I was laying in that bed, I could watch Cade take a shower … My own private show.

The very thought caused my nipples to harden and I knew if I didn't get back downstairs and out of this loft, I was going to do something drastic.

"Um … dinner?" I stuttered lamely, then nearly fainted when Cade said, "Later, there's something else I need to taste first."

# Chapter 17

*Oh. My. God! Did he just say that?*

Cade's hands gently grazed my skin as they moved up my bare arms to the straps of my tank top, causing my brain to pop, then shut off as my senses began to take over. Cade eased the straps down my arms and I felt his lips touch my shoulder ever so softly as the silky material slid down my torso, leaving my pretty purple bra exposed.

I couldn't deny that *this* was where I was hoping tonight would lead, so I'd been sure to put on my sexy underwear and shave every possible surface of my body.

Cade turned me to face him as he lowered his head and ran the tip of his tongue along the soft swell of my breasts. I murmured my approval as I freed my hands from the shirt at my waist and brought them eagerly to his biceps.

Greedy to touch him, my hands roamed over his arms, shoulders, and neck, before reaching back to pull the rubber band out of his hair, and finally doing what I'd wanted to since I'd met him.

I sunk my fingers into his dark, curly waves, loving the soft, lush feel of his hair.

His tongue dipped beneath the lace of my bra, wetting the already hard nipple, causing my head to fall slightly back and my hands to fist in his hair.

His groan mingled with my own and I moved my hands out of his hair and down to grasp the hem of his shirt in my hand, lifting it in an effort to get it off. Cade pulled it quickly over his head and I barely had time to glimpse the glorious expanse of his heavily muscled chest before he yanked the cups of my bra down and suckled my nipple into his mouth.

"You're good with that thing," I muttered, not really sure what I was saying, just that I wanted his tongue, lips, and teeth to continue doing what they were doing to my happily swollen breasts.

I reached around to undo the clasp of my bra and let it fall to the floor, then touched my palms to his hot skin and tried to read his abs like braille. The next thing I knew, his forearm was behind my ass, lifting me up, his lips moving up my neck and sucking as he maneuvered us back toward the bed.

Cade settled me back against the headboard, but I was too busy trying to fuse my lips to his neck to pay attention to what he was doing. I didn't realize he'd lifted my arm until I felt something wrap around my wrist, securing it above my head. I turned to notice it was a black nylon rope of some sort, as he lifted my other hand and secured it to the other side.

"Um…" I managed, unsure of how I felt about being tied to his headboard, when Cade's lips brushed mine, his black eyes on me as he whispered, "Trust me."

*Wow, we were really jumping right into it…*

Honestly though, if he looked at me like that and asked me in his sexy voice, I'd probably agree to dance naked down main street. So, I tried to focus on the descent of his head, rather than on the ties at my wrists.

The rough whiskers of his beard on my belly were oddly erotic and I realized I'd never been with a man who had facial hair before. My ex-husband shaved every morning, whether he worked or not.

I looked down and saw Cade's large hands working my pants and underwear down my legs and all thoughts of *The Douche* fled my mind. His dark eyes hit mine as he put one leg over his shoulder, then the other, and brought his hands to my ass and lifted. As my body came up off the bed, my fingers tried to grip the ropes and my stomach dipped nervously as I was completely suspended in air.

Cade lowered himself until he was eye level with my hips and my legs were rested along the length of his back, then I watched as his lips closed around me and his tongue began its exploration.

All worry about this unfamiliar position left me as Cade's lips, tongue, and facial hair pleasured me. My head fell back between my suspended arms and I turned myself fully over to the pleasure, not caring about anything but finding release; at the same time I wished the moment would last forever.

Too soon I felt the pressure build and my legs began to quiver as my hips thrust into Cade's mouth of their own accord.

Sensing I was close, Cade sucked my clit in his mouth, flattened his tongue and flicked it rapidly against me. I came with his name on my lips, my body trembling as I tumbled back down to earth.

My butt hit the bed as he shifted out from under me and I barely registered my hands being released from their restraints as I curled up on his bedspread, sated and happier than I'd been in years. I heard rustling, then felt Cade's heat behind me, slowly coming out of my haze when the rock-hard length of him throbbed against my backside and his lips hit my shoulder.

Suddenly not tired in the least, I turned toward him, looking down to take in the full glory of him.

My eyes bulged when I saw what he was packing in those jeans and unwittingly I said, "Holy fuck!"

Cade chuckled against the top of my head, then his breath caught when I wrapped both of my hands around him. Moving them both up and down in exploration, I worried that I'd literally break in two if he tried to impale me with it.

I mean, I knew he was a really big dude, but this was ridiculous.

Getting into my discovery of what had to be the largest cock in the free world, I stroked one hand up and down at the base, as the other toyed with the head, my eyes watching with open curiosity.

The noises coming from Cade's chest at my thorough evaluation were causing the fire within me to reawaken, and I knew I was already wet again, I just didn't know if I'd ever be wet enough to fit him inside ... Maybe if we had the sexual equivalent to a shoe horn or something.

"If you keep doing that, I'll never make it inside you," Cade growled from above me.

I tipped my head back to look up at him and replied, "Maybe it's better this way ... I'm not sure our equipment is compatible."

It started with a smile, then Cade burst out laughing and dropped a kiss on my forehead.

"Shit, Lila, only you could make me laugh when I want to fuck you so hard it's not funny."

I gulped audibly at the thought of him *fucking me so hard*, my hands still stroking as I suggested, "Maybe we can make sure you fit, before we do anything *hard...*"

Cade rolled me so I was on my back and he was over me, then lowered his head and, still smiling, said, "Don't worry, we're going to fit. I have a feeling you were made for me."

And as those words warmed my heart and soul, Cade eased himself slowly inside, giving me a chance to adjust to each inch, until he was fully seated within me. I'd never felt so complete in my life.

With Cade filling me, his weight above me and his sweet words playing like a loop in my head, I brought my knees up and savored the moment.

Cade kissed me softly and started to move. The long length of him thrusting in and out. Slowly at first, then faster, harder, longer … until his grunts were mingling with my moans.

When Cade paused, I was about to protest, then he lifted one leg and the other, until my ankles were hugging his ears and he was sitting erect. My eyes roamed, taking in his slickened chest and abs, the muscles bunching and straining as he pounded in and out of me, the visual causing my orgasm to build again.

My muscles protested as they stretched in their new position, and I thought briefly that next time I'd need to do a warm-up before sex with Cade. He began hammering into me even harder and I looked up to see the pleasure on his face as he began to come. It was enough to push me over the edge and I called out his name as I took in his expression, memorizing it for my personal masturbation reel.

A little while later, after I was back in my clothes and Cade was getting cleaned up, I grabbed my phone and covertly sent a text to Amy May.


DEED'S DONE. **It was MAGNIFICENT!**

# Chapter 18

I was replaying the reel in my head a few days later, my eyes starting to glaze over, when the sound of Elin shouting, "*Mom!*" brought me out of my dirty musings. By the look on his and Elena's faces, he must have been trying to get my attention for a while.

I picked up my neglected taco and asked, "What's up, bud?" before taking a bite.

"Look, I can do the *shocker!*" he replied, holding up his hand to show me that his thumb was holding on to his ring finger.

I sucked in a breath, stunned, causing a piece of taco shell to lodge in my throat.

Choking, I reached for my water and sucked it back in between deep breaths, my eyes watering as I looked at my son in horror.

"Don't do that," I screeched when I had the ability to speak again.

Elin's face dropped and he put his hand in his lap.

"Why, does it mean something bad?"

Not willing to explain *the shocker* to my ten-year-old son, I replied vaguely, "All you need to know is that it means something only adults need to know about and I don't ever want you to do it again, okay?"

Elin exchanged a confused look with his sister, who simply shrugged and kept right on eating as if I hadn't just almost died at the dinner table.

"Promise?" I urged when he didn't say anything.

"Okay, Mom, I promise," he said, eyes on his plate and I knew I'd hurt his feelings when he left his favorite meal untouched and asked softly, "May I be excused?"

"Sure," I replied, and watched with worried eyes as he cleared his plate and went to his room.

I sighed and looked at my daughter, unsure of whether or not she'd have questions about what just happened, but she just picked up a fallen black olive, popped it in her mouth, and asked, "Can Candace come over this weekend?"

*The Douche* and Mary were going out of town, so the kids were with me this weekend.

"Sure, honey," I replied.

"Yay! Thanks."

Once the table was cleared, the dishes were done and I figured Elin had enough time by himself, I headed toward his room, trying to figure out what I could say to ease the hurt I'd caused earlier.

My mind was preoccupied; that's why it took a moment for the scene before me to register when I opened his door.

Elin was sitting at his desk, the computer his dad had gotten him for Christmas powered up and on the screen was a naked woman. She was spread eagle and moaning, as the man laying next to her gave her *the shocker*.

I looked from the screen to my son, my horror quickening when I saw his face was rapt on the couple and his hand was down his pants.

One second, all I could hear was the low moans of the woman on the screen, the next, the room was filled with the screams of my son and me.

"*Oh. My. God!*"

"*Mom! Get out!*"

It took a minute to shake myself out of my frozen state, then I whirled and ran out of the room, shutting the door behind me as I fled.

"Oh my god…" I kept muttering it over and over until I was safely in my room.

For some reason, my room didn't seem far enough removed from the mind-blowing situation. I passed through my bathroom, into my walk-in closet, shutting the door behind me as I dropped to the floor and crawled behind my hanging clothes. I let my back hit the wall, drew my knees to my chest and held them tightly with my arms, rocking back and forth.

When had this happened? When had my sweet little boy started talking about sex and touching himself? When had he started watching porn?

"Ahhhh," I moaned as I mourned the loss.

I wasn't sure how long I sat there, purging my emotions as I came to terms with the fact my son would never be my little boy again.

I took a deep breath, stood up, and left the sanctity of my closet, then wondered what the hell my next move was supposed to be.

I moved to where my phone was charging on my dresser and picked it up, scrolling through the names until I found the one I wanted.

Luckily, I'd had the courage to finally ask Cade for his phone number before I left his house after we'd had sex – unprotected sex at that.

Yeah, so *that* happened. And it was more magical than I'd ever imagined … other than the unprotected part, which had been an oversight on both of our parts. Something I'd been wondering how to bring up the next time I saw him…

"Wilkes."

His rough voice soothed me, even as it caused my belly to dip.

"Hey, Cade, it's Lila … Do you have a minute?"

"Yeah, darlin', what's up?"

"Um, well, at dinner my ten-year-old son showed me how he learned how to do *the shocker*, then I walked in on him watching a video about it and masturbating."

I heard his deep chuckle, then he muttered, "Never a dull moment."

"*Cade*," I tried not to screech, but I felt the panic clawing at my throat again. "He's *ten*."

"It's natural, Lila, nothing to freak out about."

"Too late … What should I do? Talk to him?"

"His dad's in the picture, right?"

"Yes."

"Good, babe, then give him a shout and let him handle it. No kid wants to talk about this stuff, but he *really* doesn't want to talk to his *mom* about it. Just tell him you're sorry you overacted and assure him it's normal, so he doesn't feel like a freak. Let his pops handle the nitty gritty."

"Okay, I think I can do that," I replied, already feeling better about the whole situation. It was a talk best had between a father and son. I'd call *The Douche* right away. "Thanks, Cade."

"Anytime, darlin'. I've gotta go, but can meet up this weekend."

"I have the kids this weekend."

"How about lunch on Friday?"

"Perfect."

"See ya."

"Okay, thanks again, Cade."

I called my ex as soon as I hung up with Cade and told him everything. He surprised me by saying he'd be right over, so I hung up and went to apologize to my son for overreacting, hoping I hadn't scarred him too terribly.

# Chapter 19

Scanning the aisles as if I'd never been in this grocery store before, I read the labels as I wandered slowly. Grocery shopping was one of my favorite things. I loved to try new items and get ideas for new dishes to try with the twins. Luckily, they weren't as picky as most kids their age and would usually try anything once.

Maybe it was just the act of shopping I liked, no matter what the merchandise was.

I was trying to decide between a coconut curry sauce and butter chicken when I heard a throat clear deliberately next to me.

I turned my head to see who was trying to get my attention and saw a pretty woman who didn't look familiar.

"Hi," I said, uncertain what she wanted.

At my greeting she grinned brightly, her whole face lighting up, and said, "Hi! I know you don't know me, but you're Delilah Horton, right?" I barely had time to nod before she barreled on. "I'm Carmen Santos and I work for the Greenswood Gazette. I'm the only woman on staff, so, of course they have me working the Lifestyles section ... *Sexists* ...

Also, I'm the youngest, so I'm in charge of the Patch, the online site for the magazine. My boss thinks the internet will never take the place of the print newspaper, so he doesn't put much stock into the site. That's okay, I'm also a blogger on my own time, and don't mind keeping the paper up to date online."

*Holy crap ... I don't think she took a breath at all,* I thought as I stood there holding the jars of sauce, my mouth slightly open.

"Anywho, I've been watching you for a while, ever since you posted those pictures of your husband and that gratuitous beaver shot all over town. I really like what you did there, sticking it to the cheaters in the world, and I'd love to interview you for the paper ... I'd also love to do an exposé of you on my blog."

Carmen paused and I wondered if this was the part where I was supposed to speak. There was so much information in what she just said I wasn't sure where to start.

She brought her venti coffee cup to her lips and took a long sip, causing me to wonder who the *hell* had given this woman coffee. She needed the energy like I needed syphilis ... *Not at all!*

"Um," I started when I realized that she was breaking for me to respond. "What did you want to interview me about? Leaving my husband?"

"No, silly," Carmen replied, pulling her long caramel hair back with her free hand, twisting it, and laying it across her shoulder. "I want to do an interview about how you went from housewife to badass vigilante."

"I'm not a vigilante," I replied, looking around for hidden cameras. Because either I was being recorded or this beautiful nut was messing with me.

"A private investigator then," she amended.

"No, not one of those either," I replied, feeling frustration rise over the fact yet *another* person had seen me out taking pictures for Moose. I guess the joke was on me, I wasn't incognito at all. It was a wonder I managed to get the drop on anyone.

"But," she began, chewing her bottom lip, her face full of confusion. "Didn't you catch the bank teller and the pawn shop owner?"

I looked around, felt pretty sure we were alone and leaned down to say, "It's not really common knowledge I did that and I'd like to keep it that way. But, no, I don't usually get involved that much. Usually I just take the pictures for my boss. I'm an investigative photographer."

The confusion cleared and her face brightened again. I took a step back when she started bouncing excitedly on the soles of her feet.

"But don't you see, you're a great role model for women. Out there kicking ass and catching bad guys in the act … What a great story! We could talk about how you went from housewife, to a camera phone beaver shot, to being an investigative photographer. That's a BIG leap! We could talk about some of the cases you solved, leaving names out of course, and how your life has changed. How you turned one terrible moment in your life to a positive one by using it to help others."

Even as her compliments warmed me, and I had to admit, I liked that she thought I was a badass, I was still thinking she was a little off her rocker.

"I don't know … I kind of like the fact that *most* of the town is clueless about what I do. I don't know if posting an exposé about it would be a good idea."

"Will you think about it?" Carmen asked, lifting her giant duffel bag of a purse and searching through it. After a few seconds she said, "*Score*," then pulled a business card out and handed it to me. "Just give me a call, text, or email when you're ready and we can set something up."

I put the coconut curry sauce back on the shelf, put the

butter chicken sauce in my basket and accepted her business card.

"Butter chicken is the bomb," she said, indicating my cart, then added, "It was great to meet you," before twirling and practically skipping down the aisle.

I was exhausted just watching her.

"You too, Carmen," I called after her, before putting her card in my back pocket and continuing down the aisle.

# Chapter 20

"Do you mind if I take Elena tonight, let her and Cassidy have a slumber party?"

I looked up from licking the buttercream frosting off the cupcake in front of me and said, "Yeah, of course, Elena would love that."

I was on my way to meet Cade for lunch, but had stopped for a little pick-me-up.

*What?* Yes, I was eating a cupcake before I met Cade for lunch, but it was the first time I'd be seeing him since the night we slept together, so I *needed* it.

When my cell phone rang and I saw it was Moose calling, I told Amy May I'd be right back and walked out of the bakery to take the call.

"What's up?"

"I need you to get this shit done … *Today!*"

I held the phone away from my ear, looking at it with horror and confusion at Moose's tone.

He was losing it.

"All right, Moose, *shit*, calm down."

"Calm down? I'll fucking calm down when you do the job I

hired you to do," he screeched over the phone and I worried for a moment that he was going to give himself a heart attack raising his blood pressure that way.

"*Okay.*"

"She's at the nail salon in twenty minutes. I want you on her like flies on shit. She moves, you move. She meets with anyone, I want it on film. She gives Hector a blow job, I want to see the fucking cum on her lips."

*Ewww…*

"You got me, Delilah? We need to shut this one down."

"Yeah, I got you, Moose, don't worry."

"We need this, Lila," he said strangely and I wondered if he was talking about the money, or something else.

As soon as I hung up with him, I called the mom of one of Elin's friends and set up a sleepover for him too. It sucked to have both kids gone when it was my weekend to have them, but I needed to get this job done and over with, so I could get Moose off my back and let the Coke Club become a less-than-fond memory.

My phone pinged, signaling a text, and I looked down to see Cade had messaged me.

SOMETHING CAME UP. **Rain check.**

EVEN THOUGH I knew it was for the best since I needed to get to work, I still felt a pang of sadness over not seeing Cade today. Then I realized both my kids would be gone tonight and replied.

NO PROBLEM. **I have to work. But maybe later tonight? My kids have plans.**

. . .

I WALKED BACK in to the bakery, told Amy May goodbye, and grabbed the rest of my cupcake to eat on the way.

MAYBE. **Contact me when you're free and I'll let you know.**

VAGUE, but it was something.

I tried to remember what state we'd left the apartment in, when the last time I'd shaved was, and whether or not I had any beer in the house, as I made my way to the salon.

Keeping my eyes peeled for Hector, I drove around the back of the salon. I didn't see the Camaro, so I kept driving and parked down the alley. I got out of the van and was just about to turn from the alley into the back parking lot when a voice filtered toward me, causing me to pause behind the dumpster.

"Yeah, babe, I got a line on a couple new sellers … Yeah, I'm gonna head out there now, get a feel for the place and for them. You got it, baby, you know me… I'll make it work."

I rose slightly to peer over the top of the dumpster, my adrenaline spiking when I saw it was my perp on the phone. It looked like I was finally going to catch a break.

She slid behind the wheel of a pretty little Beemer and as soon as she shut the door, I took off toward my van.

I caught her turning onto Main Street, keeping a few car lengths behind as I tailed her out of town. I doubted she had any reason to suspect she was being followed, but although she seemed like an idiot to me, I didn't want to make assumptions and screw this up. So I was hanging back.

We were about twenty miles out of town when I began to

wonder where the hell we were heading, thirty when I wondered if this even had to do with the drugs, and forty when I thought about just turning around and heading back.

Then she turned right.

When I got to the road she turned on, I saw a sign that read, **Custom Motorcycles and Service**. Seeing her tail-lights just before they went out of view, I turned to follow.

She was parking in a lot and exiting her car, so I backed up behind the tree line, hoping it was enough to cover the car long enough for me to get a closer look. My only hope was that no one else came down the empty road anytime soon, although if they did, I'd pretend to be lost.

I stayed along the trees, watching through the branches as the perp walked through the lot, gravel crunching under her high-heeled boots and I fleetingly thought she looked like a fish out of water walking up to the motorcycle shop.

Then I stopped thinking at all as I watched Cade come out of the double steel doors and head straight for the buxom blonde, his hands circling her tiny waist as she looked up at him.

# Chapter 21

On autopilot, I took pictures as I walked through the trees, rounding the bend and getting closer to the couple in front of me.

I couldn't take my eyes off of them.

A bear could literally stop next to me to shit in the woods and I still wouldn't be able to peel my eyes away from the sight of Cade's dark head leaning down to the cokehead's fair one.

Pain clawed at my insides, yet still I moved on, shutter clicking away as I documented the worst moment of my life.

Now, that may seem a tad dramatic. I had, after all, caught my husband eating out a skank in his car; however, in this moment, I would swear to anyone who asked that I'd never felt this betrayed. This *hurt*.

Until the next moment, when the sound of Cade's voice reached my ears.

"C'mon, darlin', let's go inside."

Like a kick to the gut, I felt that *darlin'* like a steel-toed boot.

Inadvertently I gasped, then slid deeper in the woods when Cade's head came up and scanned the trees.

"*Fuck*," I whispered, peeking through the branches and

letting out a deep breath when I saw him guiding her toward the building, his hand on her lower back.

"That son of a bitch," I seethed as I headed back to my car. I knew I wouldn't get any closer to what I assumed was the MC compound than I already had. And even if I could, I wasn't sure my heart could withstand the sight of what Cade and that bleached-blonde bitch were bound to be doing once they got inside.

I'd just opened my car door when it slammed shut.

My heart pounding in terror, I turned to see Cade standing above me. Forgetting what I'd just seen, I was about to sigh in relief that it was him and not some other scary biker, when he growled, "What the *fuck* are you doing here?"

That put my back up.

"*What the fuck am I doing?* What the fuck are *you* doing, you dirty lying prick?" I asked, putting my hands to his chest and shoving with all my might.

He didn't move an inch.

"Calm down, get in your car and get the fuck out of here. I'll be by later," he said, his face inches from mine.

"Oh, *hell no,*" I seethed, literally seeing red for the first time in my life.

I'd always wondered what that expression meant. Now I knew.

"Hell, *yes,* Lila, get out of here. You'll fuck everything up if anyone sees you," he said, his face softening as he lifted his hand to touch me.

I flinched and he dropped his hand.

"Why should I believe anything you say?"

"Because you can trust me."

"*Bullshit,*" I replied softly, my rage quickly turning to devastation. I had to get out of there before I embarrassed myself by blubbering all over his chest. "I'm *going,* but I'm leaving because I don't want to be anywhere near you, *not* because you told me to."

"Whatever gets you out of here," he replied, pissing me off again. "I'll be by later."

"Don't be … I won't let you in."

Cade didn't reply, he simply waited until I got in my car and started down the lane, before turning and heading back toward the compound. I only knew this, because I couldn't stop myself from watching him in the rearview mirror.

"*Stupid fucking men,*" I muttered as I drove back to town. Then I screamed a bunch of much nastier things in Cade's honor, with the windows rolled down and the music blaring through my speakers. "*Fucking, mother-fucking, dick-sucking, lying, asshole…*"

You get the idea.

I did not go home, I did not pass go, I drove straight to Amy May's and walked into the back door of the bakery.

"Uh-oh," Amy May said when she looked up and saw my tear-ravaged, rage-filled face.

I didn't reply, instead I headed into her office and threw myself down on her flower-patterned love seat.

A few minutes later, I heard Amy May's footsteps and thrust my hand out without looking up. Once it was filled with a cupcake, I pulled it back and dove in to the fudgy goodness.

She got me a fudge cupcake with dark chocolate frosting. Amy May so got me.

"What's going on?" Amy May asked from somewhere beside me. "I haven't seen you look this crazed since you found *The Douche* behind Starbucks."

I told her everything in between bites, holding the tears at bay as I let the rage take over. When I'd finished my story, I looked up to see Amy May looking at me thoughtfully.

"What?"

"I think you should talk with him, let him explain."

"*What?*" I practically screeched.

"Look, Lila, what happened with your marriage sucked, totally, and you were one thousand percent in the right to do what you did after you found them … but, Cade isn't your ex. This isn't history repeating itself."

"It sure as hell looked like it was."

"I think you need to give him a chance to explain," she repeated, then placed her hand on my thigh as she came to sit next to me. "Everything you said about him up to this point has been great. Amazing, in fact. I can't believe he was putting you on. There has to be more to it."

"But I saw it with my own eyes," I argued, a little miffed that my best friend wasn't taking my side.

"You also thought you saw Jason with another woman, *with your own eyes*, and you were mistaken," Amy May pointed out gently. "Just hear him out."

"I'll think about it," I grumbled, then stood to leave.

"Do you want to come over, talk some more?"

"Nah, thanks, I think I'm just going to head home. Maybe take a bath."

"Want some cupcakes for the road?" she asked, and I instantly forgave her lapse in judgment.

# Chapter 22

I dried off, threw my robe on and, thinking a glass of wine was just what the doctored ordered, padded out to the kitchen. I had music playing in the bathroom while I took a bath, the strains of it filtering through my apartment so it wasn't totally still.

I placed the already opened bottle of red on the counter, then reached for my favorite goblet when Cade's voice behind me caused me to jump.

"You ready to talk?"

I whirled, my hand clutching my chest.

"*What the fuck?* How did you get in here?"

Cade was sitting at my kitchen table, legs casually stretched out before him, his hands behind his head. He was wearing a white V-neck, had cuffs and bracelets on his arms, and his hair was hanging loose with a beanie on his head.

I was trying hard to hold on to the fact that I was pissed at him. It was difficult, when all I wanted to do was lick him.

"Cade, seriously, you broke into my house? What the hell?" I asked, finding my anger.

"I told you we needed to talk and you weren't answering your phone or the door, so I let myself in."

I crossed my arms and glared at him.

"*Fine*, you want to talk?" I asked, uncrossing my arms and placing them on my hips. "Did you fuck her?"

Cade's face darkened and he sat up, no longer relaxed.

"No. I told you in the beginning that when I'm with you, I'm with only you. Don't question that shit again."

*Is he seriously getting pissed with me?*

"I saw you with your hands on the cokehead, and you told *me* to leave … What was I supposed to think?"

"You're supposed to trust what I tell you."

"How can I trust what you tell me when you've obviously been lying to me."

"I haven't lied," Cade argued, standing and moving closer so he towered over me.

Damn the man was imposing.

"Omitting shit is lying, Cade."

"*Darlin'*," he began and I felt a sharp stab in my belly.

"Don't call me that," I pleaded softly, lifting my face to his. "I heard you call *her* that and it may be stupid, but I thought the endearment was just for me. You ruined it."

I didn't care if I sounded like a petulant child, he'd hurt me.

His face clouded and he lifted a hand as if to touch me, but I backed away before he could.

Cade clenched his jaw and said, "I may not have told you everything, but what I didn't share was club business."

"What kind of business? Have you been *working* the entire time we've been together?"

"Let's just say we have a mutual interest in Hector, the Coke Club, and the man who hired you and Moose to get dirt on them."

My jaw dropped and my heart constricted painfully.

"You *have* been lying to me this whole time."

"No, Red, look…"

"Don't call me that," I said sharply, having no problem finding my inner bitch now. I was pissed. "Only my dad calls me Red. Forget the endearments, since it's all obviously been bullshit. You can call me Delilah, or Lila, or better yet, don't call me anything and get the hell out."

"Stop jumping to conclusions and listen," Cade said angrily. "What I said about seeing you on the street and everything since we met has been true. Yes, I kept my reasons for being on the street that first time I gave you a ride from you, but that's because it was club business and you didn't need to know."

"What exactly do you do for your *motorcycle gang*?" I asked snottily.

Cade's face conveyed that he was losing his patience, but I wasn't ready to give up my snit yet.

"It's a *club*, not a gang and I'm a man who gets things done."

"What the hell does that mean?"

"It means if someone's fucking with the club, I fuck with them. If there's shit going down that's bad for business, I put a stop to it. If some asshole is bringing drugs to my town and trying to get bitches to sell that shit on my compound, I do what it takes to make that shit stop."

"Including fucking me?" I asked, and unfortunately, the hurt beat out the anger and I knew Cade heard it when his face softened and he took a few steps until he was an inch from me.

"No, Lila," he said gently. "You weren't part of the plan, but the minute I saw you, I knew no matter what happened with the job, I had to have you."

"*Really?*" I wanted so badly to believe him.

His dark eyes took me in and he said, "I really like this look."

I brought my hand up to the hair piled messily upon my head, as I looked down at my bare feet and robed body and asked, "You do?"

Cade nodded and I realized the look on his face was sparking something other than anger within me.

"Yeah," he said gruffly, lowering his head inch by inch. "This look, paired with you bitchin' at me … it works for me."

Before I could reply, or protest, his lips were on mine and it was *on like Donkey Kong*.

Suddenly his lips and hands were everywhere and the adrenaline that had been pumping within me since I'd seen him earlier made every touch feel magnified. I was burning from within and was doing my best to set him ablaze as well.

My robe was gone, a pool at my feet, leaving me naked in my kitchen as Cade's adept fingers explored every inch of me. I was panting unabashedly as I tried to give as good as I was getting, running my hands along the length of his hard cock beneath his jeans.

"You want that?" Cade asked roughly in my ear, his teeth grazing my lobe lightly.

"*Yes*," I moaned. "I want it."

"Tell me…"

"I want your cock inside me," I begged, my brain turning to mush as his fingers found me.

"You're so wet for me," he said, his words only getting me hotter. "How do you want my cock?"

"Hard … Fast…"

The next thing I knew, I was bent at the waist, the hard wood of my dining room table cool beneath my breasts and stomach. I heard Cade unzip his fly, his hands continuing to work me over.

I groaned loudly as his fingers fucked me, but it wasn't enough.

"Hurry," I urged, and when I felt him rub the head of his cock along my wetness, I pushed my hips back eagerly.

Cade put one hand on my hip and the other ran up the length of my spine, then loosened my hair from its bun and tangled in it.

"Pull it," I demanded, wanting everything Cade could give me. Things I'd been afraid to ask for before, but had always fantasized about.

Cade tugged my hair, pulling me up so I had to brace my hands on the table, then slid slowly inside of me.

"Like that?"

"Harder."

Cade pulled harder, then leaned forward and bit my shoulder before pulling out and pounding back into me.

"*Yes…*"

I braced as Cade pounded, pushing my hips back to meet his every thrust, the feel of him moving inside me, along with the sweet pain of him pulling my hair, causing my breath to come out in gasps as I reached for my release.

"Touch yourself," he demanded, grunting as he moved even faster.

I caressed my breast, feeling the fullness in my palm before pinching my nipple and tugging, then I ran my hand along my stomach, down to my clit. I knew it would take no time at all; I was totally primed and ready to come apart.

"So fucking perfect," Cade murmured in my ear, biting me on the shoulder again, causing me to call his name as I came. He was right there with me and a few moments later I fell to the table, trying to catch my breath as I enjoyed the feel of the cool wood beneath me.

Meals at this table were never going to be the same…

# Chapter 23

"Um ... we just had unprotected sex ... *again*."

That was the first thing out of my mouth when I came out of the bathroom after washing up and putting my robe back on. I'd left my hair down, falling in big, sexy, I-just-had-great-sex waves around my shoulders.

Cade was sitting on my bed. He'd taken off his shirt and his cuffs, beanie, and bracelets were on my dresser. I thought this was strange, since he'd been fully clothed while we had sex.

Why take stuff off now?

He must have seen me looking at his things on my drawer, then staring at his beautiful naked chest, because he asked, "It's okay if I stay?"

I stared at him, mouth open, because for some reason the thought of him staying, and sleeping with me in my bed, hadn't crossed my mind. I'd assumed he'd want to go home.

"What about Rufus?"

"I stopped home and let him out before I came here. He'll be fine until morning."

"Oh," I replied, unsure of what else to say. Then I realized he was still waiting for me to answer, so I added, "Um ... sure, you can stay."

Then I looked at my sad little queen-sized bed and wondered how we'd both fit.

"I never have unprotected sex ... *ever*. But I've been tested by the doc and I'm clean."

It took a minute for my mind to catch up and realize he was answering my initial question.

"Oh, well, um, I was tested after I found out about my ex and I haven't been with anyone since him so ... I'm clean too."

Cade grinned and asked, "You on the pill?"

I was, due to irregular periods and horrible cramping, but rather than explaining why, I just answered, "Yes."

"Good," he said, then rose and walked to me, his hands coming to the belt at my waist. "Because now that I've had you bare, I don't want you any other way." My belly tingled, then caught fire when he added, "Sleep naked," as he tugged at my belt and pushed the robe off my shoulders.

Once we were both naked, I turned off the lights and got into bed, then laid there stiff, unsure what to do next. I relaxed when Cade's arm came around me and pulled me to him, so we were wrapped up in each other.

I'd never slept naked before, but skin to skin with Cade's heated body, it felt decadent, sinful.

He rubbed slow circles on my back and I quickly felt myself dozing off.

I had no idea how long I slept, but it was still pitch black when I woke with a moan as Cade slid inside me. He took me slowly, gently, in the dark. And I felt something shift in my heart as I came sweetly beneath him.

When I woke up the next morning, I worried things might be awkward; instead it was as if we spent the night together all the time.

Cade got up first and started the coffee, and while he was

in the shower, I made bacon and eggs. Then we sat down and ate together. It was all very normal and civilized, until I looked at the table and got flashes of what we'd done in this spot the night before.

I cleared my throat and looked up to see Cade grinning knowingly at me.

*Busted.*

Needing to talk about something else I said, "I'm supposed to give Moose the pictures from yesterday. He's been really tense lately and is adamant the client needs them right away."

"Give them to him."

"But, you're in them. So's your compound."

"I want his client to know we're looking into the situation as well, we're not too fond of Hector polluting the area with his shit and we have no intention of letting him sell here. So, give the client the pictures and let him know I'll be in touch."

"Okay."

"And be careful. If you run into Hector or the Coke Club again, I want to know about it. Watch your back and don't put yourself into a situation you can't get out of."

"Okay," I repeated, my heart warming at the fact that he was worried about me.

Shit, even with everything that had happened yesterday, it seemed I still trusted this guy and worse, I was really falling for him.

I needed to have a girl's night. Talk with my friends and sort my head out. See if they thought I was moving too fast.

"You good?" Cade asked, proving once again he could read me like a book.

"Do you think, maybe, we're going a little too fast?" I asked, lifting my mug of coffee to my lips, just to have something to do with my hands.

"Darlin'," he began, and I flinched. "I'm thirty-eight years old. I've never been in a relationship with a woman. Shit, I've never cared enough about a woman to even take her out on a date, until you. Now, I figure, I've waited a long time and I know what I want. What I want is you … so, no, I don't think it's going too fast. I think it's taking too damn long. I know where I'm at, I'm just waiting for you to catch up."

I was still trying to let that penetrate when he continued.

"And, Lila, there's times when a word's just a word, and other times when it comes from the heart. Sometimes I call people darlin' to charm them, or get what I want, but when I say it to you, it's from the heart. You asked me to stop, but I can't promise I will, because that's who you are… *My darlin'*."

My eyes widened and I gulped audibly, putting the cup down with shaky hands as I tried to wrap my head around everything he'd just laid out for me.

*Holy shit*, things were moving even faster than I thought.

"Look, I gotta go let Rufus out, then get some shit done, so I'll give you some time to think things through. You know how to get ahold of me when you're ready."

"Okay," I said again, thinking I really needed to learn to expand my vocabulary when I was around this guy.

Cade stood and dropped a kiss on my forehead before taking his dishes to the sink, grabbing his things, and leaving my apartment. Through it all, I sat at my table, my hands still wrapped around my mug as I tried to process everything that had happened since Cade rode into my life.

# Chapter 24

The rest of the weekend went by quickly.

I spent some much-needed snuggle time with my kiddos, laying around watching superhero flicks and eating lots of junk food. And happily, the awkwardness between Elin and me was gone. We'd moved on from *the incident* and were back in our comfortable mommy/son place.

I'd sent the photos to Moose and gave him the message from Cade and had blissfully heard nothing from him for three days. After the way he'd been acting lately, I was beginning to wonder whether working for him was such a good idea. I didn't need anyone yelling at me, certainly not some crabby-ass shut-in, who used me to do all of his dirty work.

On Thursday morning, I received another text from Moose telling me Hector and the cokehead were unloading merchandise and storing it at the storage place downtown, and the last thing he needed from me for this case were pictures of the drugs. After that, the client would have all the evidence he needed to shut Hector's operation down.

Eager to be done with Hector, the Coke Club, the client,

*and* Moose, I shot him a text back saying I'd get the photos, and that we needed to talk.

That's why I was currently skulking around dusty old storage units, rather than helping Amy May at the bakery.

"*I'm so done with this shit*," I muttered as I stepped in a puddle. Of course, it had to be raining on the day I'd busted out my cute new ankle boots, which were now covered in mud.

I looked around the corner to the row where Moose told me they'd be, and saw Hector's Camaro with the trunk open and no one around. Figuring they were inside the unit, and hoping there were still drugs in the trunk so I could get the picture and get the hell out of there, I ran from my hiding spot to the car, camera at the ready.

When I rounded the car and looked down, I was relieved to see there were piles of drugs still in the car. Large plastic bags full of pills, white substances and an off-white powder.

I quickly took a bunch of pictures and was getting ready to rush back the way I'd come, when a voice behind me said, "You just keep showing up."

I turned to see Hector standing precariously close, and was about to run when he grabbed my arm. Squeezing tightly, he shook me and asked, "Who the fuck are you? Who are you working for?"

My mind raced as I kept my arm with my camera behind my back and tried to wrestle my arm from his grip. It was no use; I could feel his fingers bruising my arm, his grip was so tight.

Instinctually, I took a step toward him, closing the distance as I brought my knee up hard and connected it with his junk.

"Fucking bitch!" he yelled as he bent to cradle himself, his fingers loosening enough for me to break free.

I didn't look to see how he was or if anyone was chasing me. I ran flat out, as if the hounds of hell were at my feet. Jumping in my car and starting it before my door had even shut behind me, I took off, fishtailing out of the storage lot and speeding down the street, grateful no one was behind me, but not willing to relax yet.

I drove straight to the police station and parked in their lot, figuring it was the safest place I could be, then shot a text to Cade, telling him everything that had just happened.

Next, I sent basically the same message to Moose, except I added that he was going to need to pay me extra due to the terror I'd just faced and that I wasn't sending him the pictures until he sent the money.

Finally, I texted Amy May and Bea, telling them I needed a Ladies' Night, *STAT*.

My phone started pinging as replies came in:

DONE. **Stop by and I'll give you the cash and get the pictures. I need them yesterday... And, Lila, don't get used to demanding shit.**

I ROLLED my eyes at Moose's reply, mentally telling him to *Go fuck himself.*

Then I opened Amy May's: **Sounds great.** Followed by Bea's reply: **Set it up tonight. I'll be there.**

Finally, I opened the one from Cade.

SHIT'S ESCALATING. **I don't like him putting his hands on you. Talk to your ex about taking the kids until this shit gets wrapped up. I want you at my cabin.**

MY INITIAL REACTION was irritation at Cade's bossiness, then I realized the merit of his demands. If Hector somehow found out where I lived and something happened to my kids, I'd never forgive myself, so sending them to their dad's was a good idea. Even if I hated the thought of being away from them, their safety came first. And the fact that Cade wanted me at his place so that he could protect me didn't suck either…

I texted everyone back, then decided I'd better call *The Douche* and tell him what was going on, rather than trying to tell him everything in a text. Then I needed to get to Moose's, get my money, and unload these photos. Finally, I needed to to have a drink with my girl's and talk all of this shit out.

Damn, I needed a vacation!

# Chapter 25

I walked up to Moose's decaying house in the *up and coming* section of Greenswood, planning to make this as quick as possible. I didn't like to be at Moose's any longer than necessary. It wasn't that he wasn't nice to me, usually, and an okay boss, it's just that something about being alone in his house with him gave me the creeps.

I walked up the cracked cement steps and pounded on the ripped screen door. I heard "Come in," shouted between a fit of coughing and wheezing.

*Oh goodie*, I thought as I opened the door. *Sounds like Moose is all phlegmy again.*

"What the hell?" I muttered as I walked into the entryway, down the hall, and through the kitchen. Moose's house was never neat and tidy, but it wasn't usually as bad as this.

Trash thrown literally on the floor, dirty dishes everywhere, and a smell I wasn't quite sure I wanted to identify assailed me as I hurried toward his back porch, where I knew he'd be stationed.

"What's going on, Moose?" I asked as I entered his makeshift office.

He turned to me and I stopped, shocked at the state he was in.

Big and tall, Moose was six foot two, three hundred pounds on a good day, but he looked like he'd gained weight since the last time I saw him. And his hair, which was balding on top, but usually kept trim on the back and sides, was long and stringy. Greasy from not being washed. His clothes were filthy, with food stains and sweat rings, and his face was ragged, as if he hadn't slept in days.

"You got the pictures?" he asked, not even looking my way.

"Yeah, but, Moose, are you okay?" I asked, pulling the card out of my camera and placing it in his offered hand.

He popped it in his computer without answering, then let out a relieved sigh when the pictures showed on his screen.

"Finally," he bit out softly. "Maybe now he'll have what he needs and move forward. Get off my back."

"Who?"

"Carlos Chavez, head of a Columbian drug cartel and older brother to Hector Chavez. He's our client."

I let that information whirl around in my head, then I grabbed Moose's meaty arm and screeched, "*What?* You took a drug lord as a client? Are you *fucking crazy?*"

"He's pissed his little brother's sneaking around behind his back, trying to start up his own business here on the side. Carlos doesn't take kindly to being played, especially by his brother, so he hired me to find out exactly what Hector is doing in town."

"And you didn't think to let me in on this little tidbit of information before you gave me the job? Shit, Moose … I have kids."

"Look, Lila, shit just got out of hand. I thought he'd be happy with the initial shots of the women Hector was targeting, but he always wanted more. He wanted to be sure of his brother's betrayal before he sends his guys up here to take care of the situation."

"Take care of the situation? What does that mean? And there are more of them coming here? What the hell are you thinking, Moose? You've gotta tell the cops."

Moose shook his head, then pulled out a canvas bag and threw it at me.

"Too late for that, Lila, the job's done. Once I send these pictures over to Carlos, he'll have the final piece he was looking for. He'll get Hector and the drugs out of Greenswood and things will get back to normal."

I opened the bag and looked inside. There were piles of cash rubber banded together. I threw it back at Moose like it was on fire and said, "I can't take that. It's *drug* money, Moose. You may have lost your mind, but I haven't. I can't believe you'd put me in danger like this."

Moose's beady eyes hit mine and he assured me, "It's fine, Lila. Carlos promised me he wouldn't touch you. He's grateful for the evidence you found. It'll be fine," he said again, and I began to wonder if he was drunk.

"No, Moose, it isn't fine. Not until Hector and Carlos are out of town and out of our lives. I'm getting my kids to safety and hiding out until this all blows over. I think you should do the same."

Not waiting for his response, I got out of there as fast as I could, shaking my head as I went over everything he'd just admitted to me.

What a *stupid fuck*!

The sad part was I didn't think I'd be able to work for him anymore, not after he pulled this shit, and I really enjoyed my job. I'd have to figure out another way to make money, something that didn't involve drug cartels and drug-dealing bimbos.

I called Bea as I drove away, telling her everything I'd just learned from Moose. She said she'd look into Hector and Carlos and put everyone at the station on alert.

"Are you sure you still want to go out tonight?" she asked.

"*Hell yeah*," I replied, desperation clear in my voice. "Moose is sending the final photos to them now and they're all the way in Columbia. Nothing's going to go down tonight and tomorrow we're all going to go off the grid for a while. I really need tonight with you and Amy May to blow off steam and have some girl talk."

"Okay, I'll see you then, and, Lila … Be careful."

# Chapter 26

"This is so lame," I whined as I picked up my dirty martini and took a sip.

"What?" Amy May asked, smiling at me over her Cosmo.

"It's six thirty on a Thursday night," I explained. "When I said I wanted a Ladies' Night, I meant go out, get drunk, stir some shit up. Not dinner and drinks and home by eight."

"We're not in our twenties anymore," Bea responded. "We all have to work tomorrow and have families at home ... We have to be responsible, not go out and get blitzed, then have to deal with the horrors of a hangover the next day."

I pouted because she had a point and that sucked.

"Hey, if it makes you feel better, we can just order appetizers. You'll get a buzz quicker that way," Amy May said, always thinking ahead.

I grinned at her and said, "Deal," then laughed. "Remember when we used to be able to stay out all night drinking, then go right to work the next day without getting any sleep?"

"Yeah, now if I don't get my full eight hours after just one glass of wine, I can't even function," Bea said sadly, and both Amy May and I nodded in agreement.

"Ugh, try running a bakery. If I'm not in bed by eight, I'm a bear in the morning. Jason says I'm worse to get up than the kids."

"Are you ladies ready to order?" the hot young waiter asked us, pulling us out of our depressing conversation.

"Can we get the spinach dip?"

"And the potato skins?"

"Oh, and those little taquito things?"

"Sure, anything else?"

"Another round, please."

"Got it … Dirty martini, Cosmo, and red wine coming up. And I'll get those apps right in for you."

"Thanks," I said, then watched his butt as he walked away.

When I turned my attention back to my friends, they were both staring at me.

"What?"

"Didn't you ask us here to tell us about Cade?" Amy May asked, taking the lime peel out of her drink and running her tongue around it in what I assumed was supposed to be a sexy move, but just came off as creepy.

"Stop doing that," Bea said, causing Amy May to drop the peel.

They were right, I did bring them there to talk about Cade, so I laid it all out. Catching Bea up on the stuff she missed, then telling them both about the night he broke in and all the stuff he said about me being the one for him and the business about calling people *darlin'*.

"I really like him; when can we go on a double date?" Amy May asked, picking up a loaded potato skin and biting it with a moan. "These are so good."

"Uh, I don't know," I replied, wondering what Cade would think about going on a double date. "That doesn't really seem like his scene. Maybe we could plan a barbecue or something … a few months from now."

"A few *months*?" she asked with a scowl.

"Could you let me get used to this first? He hasn't even met my kids or anything yet and I was the first person he ever dated … I'd like to hold off on throwing him into the fire with my friends."

Bea hadn't said anything, so I turned my attention to her and asked, "What are you thinking?"

"I'm not sure yet, the jury's still out."

"Why?" Amy May asked.

"Because, Amy May, the fact that he's a *man who gets things done* kind of freaks me out. I'm not positive he's on the right side of the law, even if this time he's working on keeping drugs out of our city. Plus, he's breaking into her apartment and bossing her around all the time. I'm not certain he's the guy for Lila, so I'm reserving judgment until I know more."

"It doesn't sound like you're reserving judgment; in fact, you sound very *judgy*," Amy May argued, and I just sat back, munching on taquitos and sipping on my martini as I watched. "He makes her feel safe. He likes her, like, *really* likes her. He's never dated anyone before, yet now he's dating *her*. He's a big mountain of Hawaiian hotness, who gets her off like no one has before, especially *The Douche*, and badass motorcycle man with a dog and a cabin. What the hell's not to like?"

"We'll just have to agree to disagree on this one, okay, Amy May?" Bea said, running her hand over her short hair and causing it to spike up. "I'm sorry, Lila, I want you to be happy, I do. I just want to make sure you're thinking with your head, not your loins."

"Her *loins*?" Amy May guffawed, falling sideways in the booth and bumping Bea's shoulder.

"Shut up," Bea said with a laugh. "You know what I mean."

"You need to stop reading those old historical romance novels," Amy May teased, and I knew their argument was over.

I was okay with the fact that Bea didn't jump on board the Pro-Cade train right away. I knew she was just looking out for me and as a cop, wanted to make sure I wasn't getting involved in anything dangerous.

Well, *more* dangerous than what I was already involved in with Moose, Hector, Carlos, and the Coke Club. I'd agreed to send her all of the pictures I'd taken so far, along with any information I could think of that Moose had given me over the course of the last few weeks.

"I will say one thing," Bea said as she finished the last of her wine. "Cade's right about the kids staying with *The Douche* and you staying with him. I'll feel better knowing you're all safe until we can find Hector and get him off the streets. Hopefully, before his brother finds him. The last thing we need is a drug war in the middle of Greenswood."

"I talked to him earlier. He's picking the kids up at the apartment after school tomorrow and then I'm going to Cade's."

"Another round, ladies?" the hot waiter asked, coming up to clear our empty plates.

"Nah, we're old," I said with a chuckle. "We have to get home and go to bed."

The waiter laughed, probably thinking I was joking, and said he'd be right back with our bill.

"Hey, how's it going?" a happy voice chimed in and we all turned to see Carmen Santos approaching the table.

Well, maybe not so much approaching as hopping. She was once again smiling happily, her long, two-toned hair straightened so that it fell almost to her waist. She was wearing a maxi skirt and a tank top, with bangles adorning her wrists.

"Hey, Carmen," I said, smiling back. I looked around to see my friends smiling at her too. So either it was because her smile was infectious, or we each had a good buzz. "These are my friends Amy May, and Bea."

Carmen gave a little finger wave, then said, "Best cupcakes in the *world* and toughest cop in town."

Amy May and Bea both practically beamed at Carmen's praise and I realized she was probably the most positive, uplifting person I'd ever met.

"Carmen's a reporter," I added, completing the introductions, although Carmen seemed to know who everyone was.

"And a blogger," she amended cheerfully. "I'd *love* to do a post about your bakery, Amy May."

"Really?" Amy May asked, obviously pleased.

"Really," Carmen mimicked. "Oh, and a piece in the Lifestyle section of the Gazette. That would be *awesome!*"

"I'd love that, thanks!"

"Sure thing! I just saw you gals over here and wanted to stop by and say, *what's up* … I'm actually on a date," she said, pointing over her shoulder toward the bar.

We all leaned in to look around her and toward the bar. There was a younger man wearing jeans, a Batman T-shirt, and a hoodie, giving us nervous glances from his stool.

"First date?" Bea asked, her nose scrunched up.

*Uh-oh,* I thought. Even though Bea didn't know Carmen, she was Bea and she'd had two glasses of wine, so it wouldn't occur to her *not* to give her opinion.

"Yeah, Jonathon," Carmen replied with a nod, her eyes on Bea. "Why?

*Now she'd done it…*

"Well," Bea started. "First of all, who wears a hoodie on a first date? The batman shirt I'll give him, but wear it under a nice jacket or blazer, with some jeans that aren't ripped. And for crying out loud, do something with your hair."

We all turned to look at Jonathon, who looked liked he'd just rolled out of bed and hadn't bothered to comb his hair, which hadn't been cut in a few months and looked poofy. And not in a good way.

"Second of all, how old is he? Twenty? He looks like a slacker and *again*, not in a good way."

"He's, ah, twenty-two, I think. Lives in his parents' basement and works for some online company."

I winced, knowing Bea was not going to be happy with his status, then all of a sudden the situation hit me and I got the giggles.

"How old are you?" Bea asked, ignoring my giggles.

"Thirty-two."

"Go, girl," Amy May said, at the same time I asked, "Really?"

I would have guessed her to be twenty-six at the oldest. The giggles fled me as I wondered how she looked so youthful and happy and she was only three years younger than me.

"I dig the younger man thing, but you can do better. A pretty woman like you with a positive attitude and a disposition that lights up the room..." Bea trailed off as Carmen's eyes widened and she looked at Bea like she was the sweetest person in the world.

"*Really?*" she whispered, and we all answered, "Really!"

Carmen graced each of us with a smile and when our hot young waiter returned, not even bothering to hide his interest in her, she said, "Well, I guess I'd better get back and let you guys go. It was good to finally meet you all. Maybe we could get together for drinks one night," she added shyly.

"That sounds great," Amy May replied.

"You got it," Bea said, then added, "And dump the loser."

The waiter smiled and I could tell he wanted to agree and apply to be her replacement date, but kept it to himself.

"I'll call you," I said, causing Carmen's light to shine on me before she turned and bounded back to the bar.

I'd said it not just because the thought of all of us having drinks sounded like a blast, but because I thought maybe I should talk to Carmen about Carlos, Hector and the Coke Club, and have her write an exposé on what the country club set had been planning to do in our town. I'd have to be kept anonymous, of course, but the town deserved to know what was going on right under its nose.

Bea and I said bye to Amy May, then Bea drove me home. Shannon had stayed with the kids while we went out, so Bea was picking her up and they were going home after dropping me off.

I had to pack the kids and my bags and I wanted some snuggle time with my babies before I told them they were going to their dad's for a while and why. I figured it was also time to bring up Cade, since I was going to be staying at his house, and with the way things were progressing, they'd probably be meeting him soon.

# Chapter 27

"I think I packed everything they should need. If not, Elena has her key to the apartment so you can come back and get what they forgot."

We were loading up my ex's Mercedes and once they were gone I was going to lock up and head to Cade's. Elena and Elin were currently walking out of the apartment building with their treasured possessions: tablets and portable gaming systems.

"Leave it open!" I shouted, not wanting to have to dig out my keys and reopen the front door after they left.

When they got to the car, I alternated giving them hugs and kisses, then let them go so they could put their stuff inside.

"I'll call you every day," I promised, wishing I didn't have to do this.

Elena rolled her eyes. I'd been fawning over them since I made it home last night and she was at the point now where she was ready to leave me. It was actually easier this way, since last night she'd protested, asking to come with me to Cade's instead of going with her dad and Mary.

"They'll be fine," my ex assured me. "Right, guys? It'll be fun … Like an extended vacation."

"Except we still have to go to school and do chores," Elin grumbled. He'd been bargaining to miss school while they were gone, but I'd said *no way*.

When my ex moved closer, my instinct was to move farther away, but I stood my ground and looked him in the eye.

"So this guy, he's only like a fling, right?"

"What?" I asked, confused by the change in conversation, and that we were having it on the street in front of my place with the children present.

"He's not your type."

"My *type*?"

My ex pointed to himself and I took in his manicured hands, nice loafers, and perfectly styled hair. Then I thought of Cade, a huge beast of a man with dangerous eyes and luscious hair. The two couldn't be more different. And not just looks either. In the way they thought, acted, and lived their lives.

I was smiling when I answered, "No, he's not a fling."

I waited for him to respond, then watched as his eyes got wide at something over my shoulder. I turned my head to see a big black van barreling toward us. It headed our way and screeched to a halt before making contact. I saw Hector and a couple of men I'd never seen jump out and run at me.

It was so much like a scene out of a movie that I didn't react at first, I just watched, stunned, as if I were looking at it happen to someone else.

Then, when it registered who it was and that they were after me, I turned back to my ex and screamed, "*Eric, get the kids out of here!*"

I saw him grab Elin, then Elena by their waists and lift them, one under each arm in a football hold, before he took off running.

When I turned back to start kicking, or scratching, hoping

to run myself, Hector was already there. Before I could do anything, two man grabbed me, each one holding an arm.

"Hey, Red," Hector said, pulling my attention to him. He lifted a hand and blew something in my face, dazing me for a second. I shook my head and noticed Eric and the kids had just entered the apartment complex and the door was slamming behind them, but I did so in a fog, not really caring.

Hector told me to get in the van, so I followed him to the open door and climbed up inside. I was seated next to one of the guys who'd helped hold me down. I looked at everyone in the van with disinterest, noting there were three guys with Hector, and that the van smelled like Burger King Whoppers.

"I've never really seen how this stuff works," the guy to my left said. I glanced over at him briefly, noting he was ugly as sin, with a sinister-looking smile.

"Unbutton your shirt," he ordered.

I lifted my hands and began unbuttoning my shirt.

Things were kind of hazy, almost like a dream, and their voices sounded like they were coming at me through a funnel.

"Stop fucking around. That's not what this is about; button your shirt back up," Hector said, and I noted that *ugly as sin* stiffened next to me, obviously upset he'd been overruled.

I changed course and began buttoning my shirt back up.

I felt a tug on my hair and turned slightly to see *ugly as sin* twirling a lock of my hair around his finger.

"Unbutton," he mouthed, barely a whisper coming out. So I changed course again and went back to unbuttoning my shirt.

This time, I finished my task then waited, my fingers holding the bottom of my shirt.

"Open it," he leaned down and whispered in my ear.

I spread the shirt open and felt his eyes on me. It didn't bother me. It didn't *not* bother me. It just was...

"Show me your tits," he said next.

As I moved to comply, the guy on the other side of me muttered, "*Jefe*," which got Hector's attention.

Hector turned around, saw what was going on in the backseat, told me "Put your shit back on," and started screaming at *ugly as sin* in rapid-fire Spanish.

I didn't know how long we'd been driving, but when my shirt was back to rights, we slowed down and then the van stopped.

"Get out."

I followed the tattle-tale guy out of the van and waited to see where we were going next.

Hector took me by the arm and led me in to an old warehouse, looked over his shoulder and gave the guy behind us some sort of instructions in Spanish and I heard a gun fire.

I glanced behind me to see what had happened and watched with disinterest as *ugly as sin* dropped to the street behind me. Dead.

Turning my head back, I let Hector guide me inside without making a peep.

We walked into the dark warehouse, through a large open area, then into an office of some sort. We kept going through another door into a large bay that was sectioned off. There was a light in the distance and we headed toward that.

When we turned the corner and into the lit space, I saw three folding chairs. One was empty. One had a gun, a saw, a sledge hammer, and pliers laying across it. And, in the last one sat a barely conscious, obviously beaten, Moose.

# Chapter 28

"What'd you do to her?" Moose asked, his voice hoarse as if he'd been yelling, or screaming.

His head was rolled to the side, his hands tied behind his back, and he had his good eye trained on me. His other was swollen shut.

Unsure of what I should do, and distracted by an overhead light that's fluorescent light kept blinking and buzzing, I stood there waiting for instruction, my attention moving from Moose to the light above me.

"Hey, Red." Hector snapped his fingers in front of my face, pulling me away from the flickering light and back to him.

"Don't call me that," I said automatically.

"I'll call you whatever the fuck I want, *bitch*, now go pick up the pliers and sit in the empty chair."

I didn't flinch when he yelled in my face, but simply moved to do what he'd told me to.

When I was in the chair, pliers in hand, I looked at him expectantly.

"Use the pliers to break your finger."

I lifted my left hand, spreading my hands out in a fan before looking back at Hector in question.

"Pointer," was his response.

Placing the pliers around my finger, I began to squeeze, feeling a faint twinge of pain. I looked back at Hector, who yelled, "Do it!"

I put more pressure on the handles as Moose started pleading, "No, no, Lila, don't do it."

"Break it," Hector ordered.

I squeezed the handles with all my might then jerked my right hand up as I pulled my left down, twisting as I did. I felt the white-hot pain at the same time I heard the satisfying sound of the bone crush beneath the pliers.

I bit back a wave of nausea and was aware of the sweat beading on my face; still, I looked up at Hector and waited further instruction.

"Good, Red," He said, and I felt the sudden urge to turn the pliers on him and take out an eye. Hector must have read my intent, because his face hardened and he bit out, "Don't even think about it. Put the pliers down."

I tossed them down, the clang of metal hitting the floor echoing in the room.

"Now, stand up and pick up the sledgehammer," Hector commanded.

I did what he said, favoring my left hand as I walked to the chair and picked up the sledgehammer with my right. I turned, holding the handle tightly, and waited.

"What are you doing?" Moose asked, his eye moving between Hector and me, before stopping to stare at the hammer in my hands, his face conveying his obvious terror. "You can't…"

"Jorge said you've been uncooperative," Hector answered, walking forward then crouching in front of Moose and waving his hand back at me. "I thought maybe your partner would be more persuasive."

"Take out his knee," Hector demanded, rising and moving to the right to give me access.

"Nooooo," Moose bellowed, and I paused.

Suddenly Hector was right in my face, his hand clenching my jaw tightly.

"You don't listen to him; you listen to me … Take out his fucking knee."

Without further ado, I lifted the sledgehammer high over my shoulder with both hands, aware of the pain in my broken finger, but still intent on following his order. I marched to Moose, swinging as I moved, and hit his knee so hard, I could hear the bone shatter seconds before he let out a blood-curdling scream.

I felt bile rise in my throat as I looked over my shoulder at Hector, sweating pouring down my face now.

"The other one," he said, taking a pack of cigarettes out of the pocket in the front of his shirt and lighting it.

"No, please, *God*, no," Moose pleaded between sobs and wheezes.

"Wait," Hector ordered.

I paused, wiping the sweat from my brow with my forearm.

"Who hired you?" Hector asked, taking a drag.

"I can't … He'll kill me."

"What the fuck do you think we're doing right now, *ese*?"

"*Lila, please*," Moose begged, trying to reason with me, even though he obviously knew I was beyond reason.

Heedless to his begging, I awaited instruction from Hector.

"You want to know the funniest part, *ese*? The shit she's on … She's going to tell me everything I want to know anyway." He looked back at me and nodded, "Do the other one."

Hector had barely finished his sentence before I was swinging back and connecting with Moose's left knee.

Screams echoed off the walls of the warehouse and I wondered absently how the entire city didn't hear Moose's pain.

"Bitch, who hired you?"

I turned my attention from Moose to Hector and said monosyllabically, "Your brother, Carlos."

Hector's rage mingled with Moose's cries filling the space as he moved, his gun aimed at Moose's head.

Moose had a moment to look at me and whisper, "*Sorry,*" before Hector unloaded the clip in his face.

Bits of blood, skin, bone, and possibly brain splattered across my face, chest, arms, and torso, yet still I stood silently holding the sledgehammer.

"Everything okay, *jefe?*" one of Hector's men asked, stepping into the room.

"Carlos is on his way," Hector managed, right before the sound of gunfire rang outside the walls.

Hector and his man ran out toward the action leaving me behind without a word.

After standing there for a moment, my eyes on the door they'd just left, I walked over to the folding chair and put the sledgehammer back where I got it. Then I went and sat in the empty chair next to it, listening to the sounds of yelling and shots being fired.

I don't know how long I sat there, with Moose's ravaged body next to me, the smell of feces and death swimming all around me. But, eventually, the sound of footsteps had me looking up from my injured hand and I saw a tall, handsome man step through the door.

He surveyed the room dispassionately then asked, "You the photographer?"

I nodded.

"Your man is on his way," he said strangely, before leaving as quickly as he'd arrived.

I waited, drifting along in a fog as I thought about absolutely nothing.

After a while, bits and pieces of clarity began to take hold of me and I began to shake.

Just a little bit at first, then more and more, until my entire body was rattling. I hugged my hands around myself to try and stave it off, but it only got worse as my senses came alive.

Next the smells in the room registered, and the magnitude of everything that had happened began to hit me. I dropped to my knees as the tears began to fall and I looked to my right.

*Moose.*

I think that's when the wailing began ... As I looked over at Moose's lifeless body, all of my focus on the knees *I* had broken, the pain I'd inflicted on the man who'd been my boss.

I was throwing up on the ground in front of me when Cade hit the room at a full sprint.

"*Mother fucker!*" he exploded, but I wasn't sure if he was talking about me or Moose, because I was still dry heaving on the floor.

I felt a presence at my back and the hair being pulled off the nape of my neck, then the heat of Cade's breath against my ear.

"*Lila, darlin' ... fuck...*"

His hand rubbed small circles on my back until I stopped heaving, then I was lifted into his arms and he was carrying me out of the warehouse as I cradled my injured hand against me.

As we neared the exit, I could hear the sound of sirens outside and I looked at Cade dazedly.

"How'd you find me?"

Cade looked into my eyes sharply and asked, "They give you something?"

I nodded, then flinched when the bright morning light hit my face.

"What time?" I managed, watching as Bea rushed toward me.

"It's about eight AM. You were taken yesterday around four, according to your ex."

Surprised, I brought my eyes to his face, taking in his beautiful features, drawn tight in angry lines, and a little more reality slipped in. Although it had felt like very little time had passed for me during the ordeal, I was obviously gone much longer than I thought.

"The twins?" I asked, suddenly filled with the terror that had evaded me for the last sixteen or so hours.

"Fine," Cade answered instantly. "Your ex has them."

"Are you okay?" Bea asked anxiously when she reached us.

I looked at my friend, my eyes filling with tears and answered truthfully, "No."

"She needs a hospital," Cade said gruffly. "You can get her statement later."

I saw Bea stiffen, obviously offended Cade would think she'd take her profession more seriously than her friend's abduction.

She looked at me her face filled with worry and rather than tearing him a new one she simply agreed, "Yeah, the ambulance is two minutes out. We'll get you checked out."

"I'm taking her," Cade replied, shooting her a look that brokered no argument.

I saw her bite her tongue again and nod, then Cade started walking, still cradling me in his arms. When we reached his truck he kissed me sweetly on the forehead before placing me gently inside.

# Chapter 29

*Beep … beep … beep…*

"I swear if that beeping doesn't stop I'm going to rip the plug out of the wall."

I'd been in the hospital for what felt like days, but was actually only hours, and still I was ready to lose my mind.

I hated hospitals. Only went to them when I absolutely had to … Namely, when I gave birth to my children and after being kidnapped by drug lords.

I was ready to get out of this sterile room with its incessant beeping, out of this flimsy gown that barely covered my ass, and away from the prying fingers and sad eyes of everyone who entered my room.

"Just a little while longer," Cade said, trying to hide his small smile unsuccessfully, which only increased my bad mood. "They want to make sure all of that shit is out of your system."

I sighed, frustrated but resigned.

The doctor had worked on my finger while I was still kind of out of it, and I now had a split keeping it straight. Because they weren't certain how it would mix with the zombie drug I'd been given, I wasn't given any pain medication yet, but they promised to send me home with some.

"I know ... I'm just ready to go," I told Cade. "I need a shower, my pajamas, and a very, very large glass of wine."

I knew I sounded whiny, but holding on to my anger and frustration was the only thing keeping me from falling apart. I was doing my best to focus on that and keep the memories of what I'd been through, *what I'd done*, at bay.

"Lila," Cade murmured, pulling me out of my head. "I want you to come to my place. At least for a few days ... Until you're back on your feet."

I was about to answer when the door burst open and my twins came dashing in, hurtling themselves onto my bed.

Eric walked in behind them and I watched wordlessly as Cade slipped out, lifting his chin at Eric as he passed him.

Eric turned, eyes on Cade as the door closed behind him, before rotating back to me and the kids.

"You okay?" he asked, coming to stand next to the bed while our kids did their best to fuse themselves next to me.

"Yeah," I lied, not wanting to scare Elena and Elin.

"Okay, guys, you know the nurse said you could only come in for a minute," Eric said.

"What?" I asked, trying to get my arms around my babies, but without wrapping all of my IVs around them or jostling my finger.

"Sorry, Lila, they aren't even supposed to be allowed on this floor, but Bea pulled in a favor."

"When can we come home?" Elena asked as her dad shifted her off the bed.

"I need you to stay with your dad for a couple more days, okay, sweetheart? Then we'll all be back together."

Neither of my children looked happy at this news, but they didn't whine or complain, they just let their father lead them out after giving me kisses and telling me they loved me.

Elin threw one last look over his shoulder and waved, then they were gone.

The very thin line I had on my control was threatening to snap, when the door opened again and Amy May came in. She was carrying an oversized purse and wearing sunglasses, and the way she was acting made me laugh in a time when I didn't think I'd be able to.

"What the heck are you up to, girl?" I asked with a chuckle.

Amy May sidled up to the bed and slid her hand inside her purse, then leaned down close to me ear as she tried to covertly hand me a cupcake.

"Salted caramel," she whispered, then hurried back to the door to keep lookout.

"*Oh my God*! I love you," I cried, then without wasting any time, I ate that cupcake like someone was about to take it from me. Because, seriously, if the nurse had come in and caught me, she would have.

Once I was licking the last bit of gooey deliciousness from my fingers, I looked at my best friend and said, "You're a goddess."

Amy May gave me a shaky smile and I demanded, "No, don't do it. You just made me feel good for the first time in twenty-four hours, please don't ruin it."

"But..."

"*Please...*"

I watched Amy May take a deep, cleansing breath, then plaster on a fake smile.

"Better?"

"Much," I said gratefully.

"Well, your Adonis outside said they're about to let you go, so I guess I'll skedaddle ... I just wanted to see for myself you're okay."

"I will be," I assured her. "I just need a little time. But, Amy May? Thanks for coming ... and for the cupcake."

Amy May gave me a nod and even though she was wearing sunglasses, I could tell she was about to break, so I didn't say anything else as she pushed open the door and left me alone.

This time when the door opened, it was the nurse coming to discharge me. I did my best to stuff the empty cupcake wrapper under my butt, but when her gaze hit mine, an eyebrow raised, I knew I was busted.

I grinned sheepishly, then listened as she went over instructions for the next couple of days.

After she left and I was finally able to dress in the sundress Bea had brought by for me on her visit, I walked out of the bathroom to see Cade standing by the door.

"Where am I taking you?" he asked, his exhaustion apparent, making me wonder if he'd slept at all since Hector had snatched me outside of my apartment building.

"I'd like to come back to your place, if that's still an option."

Cade's face cleared and I took his offered hand.

"I wouldn't have it any other way, darlin'."

# Chapter 30

I made it all the way to Cade's couch before I completely lost it.

We'd driven in relative silence, which meant my mind had the opportunity to wander, *to remember.*

I'd jumped down from his truck and walked to his front door with visions of Moose blurring my vision. I could actually feel the weight of the sledgehammer and hear his kneecap bust as I hit it with full force.

I sprawled on the couch, tears streaming down my face, as sobs began to rack my body. I felt the cold wetness of Rufus's nose pushing on my arm, then I was being lifted as Cade sat on the couch and settled me in his lap.

His arms held me tight and I burrowed in, my nose in his throat as I bawled.

"Get it out," Cade said against my hair, his hand doing those wonderful circles on my back again.

"I busted Moose's kneecaps," I wailed miserably.

"I know, darlin', I'm sorry."

"He begged me not to do it, and his screams … *God, Cade, his screams* … Before Hector shot him, Moose told me he was sorry…" I was rambling, but he told me to get it all out, so I was.

"He was sorry for pulling you so deep into shit that heavy," Cade assured me.

I nodded against him.

"That shit was so crazy, Cade," I said, pulling back so I could look at him. "While I was on it, it was like I didn't care. Not about anything. They could tell me to do anything and I would have."

Cade reached back, pushing his pelvis up off the couch so we both rose slightly, as he grabbed something. When we settled back down, he reached his hand out and said, "Here."

I looked down at the white fabric, confused. Then, when it hit me what it was, I got a big grin on my face.

"You carry a handkerchief?"

Cade's lip tipped up, his eyes roaming my face and I knew I must look a huge snotty mess. I grabbed the hanky out of his hand and brought it to my face.

Once I, hopefully, looked a little less haggard I said, "Thanks," then waved the hanky in front of him with an eyebrow raised.

"My mom says a gentleman always carries a handkerchief."

If you would have asked me five minutes earlier if I had it in me to laugh, I would have said, *hell no*, but the serious look on Cade's face when he said that sentence had me *rolling*.

I was leaning into him again, shaking in his arms, but this time it was because I was guffawing as I tried to speak.

"You, badass biker who lives in a cabin with his crotch-sniffing dog, doing what needs to be done and answering no questions … *You* carry a hanky?"

I was laughing so hard I didn't notice he was annoyed until he said, "Keep up the jokes and I'll bend you over and tan that ass."

*What?* That made me sit up and listen.

No longer laughing, I asked somewhat breathless, *"Really?"*

"Jesus," Cade replied, all signs of annoyance gone. "You're a piece of work."

"So, does that mean no spanking?" I asked with a straight face, then lost it when I started to giggle.

With a frustrated growl, Cade lifted me off his lap and put me on the couch next to him, then got up and walked into the kitchen.

"Uh-oh, Rufus, I think I made your daddy angry," I joked, reaching out to pet Rufus's ginormous head.

A few minutes later Cade turned on the TV, sat back down, and handed me a healthy goblet of wine.

"Figured you could drink that and relax, then do the shower and pajamas thing, unless you want to shower now…"

I looked from the beautiful red liquid to the beautiful man next to me, and replied, "I'll relax first."

He nodded and settled in, putting his arm over the back of the couch so I could scoot back and fit in the crook of his arm. When *The Heat* came on, he put the remote down and I curled my feet up under me, then we sunk back in the cushions and laughed while Melissa McCarthy gave Sandra Bullock a hard time.

Feeling loosey goosey after two goblets of wine and two hours of laughter, Cade helped me up to his loft. When we got to the top, he pushed me gently toward the shower and started to the bed.

"You aren't going to join me?" I asked.

"Lila, you've been through a lot."

"Yeah … that's why I need you to wash my back," I said coyly, starting to take my clothes off and hoping he wouldn't reject me. After the ordeal I'd been through, I felt fragile, and really needed to know that he would comfort me, however I needed it.

Cade must have read what I was feeling on my face, because he crossed to me to help me out of the dress and turned on the shower. I stepped into the steaming stream as I watched him take off his shirt, then his pants, and let his hair down, then join me and close the glass around us.

"C'mere," he said, reaching for his shampoo and turning me so he could lather it in my hair. I placed my uninjured hand against the glass for support, moaning at how good it felt to have him massaging my scalp.

When he was done he turned me to rinse it out, then added conditioner. I peeked at the bottles, curious as to what brand he used, since his hair always looked so lush, then closed my eyes again and enjoyed the pampering.

Other than his hands cleaning my body, the shower was PG-13, but once we were done I felt a thousand times better.

He wrapped me in a fluffy towel, his hands moving vigorously as he dried me off. When he was finished, I curled into him and said, "Thanks ... *really*, for everything, Cade. For coming after me, taking care of me, making me laugh." I tipped my head back and looked up at his gorgeous dark eyes and admitted, "I don't know how I would have got through all this without you."

I reached up to kiss him. Softly, slowly, thoroughly. My head tilted and his large hand came up to cup the back of my head. The towel fell to the floor and I pressed my naked body against his.

"Lila," Cade said in warning, and I knew he was worried it was too soon.

The desire coursing through me reminded me I was alive and well, and that was exactly what I needed, so I looked him in the eyes and pleaded, "I need this. I need you."

Saying no more, Cade swept me up off my feet and carried me to his big comfy bed, laying me on the bed as if I was delicate, precious, before covering me with his strength.

When he slid inside me, staring into my eyes as his finger gently traced my lips, my eyes filled with tears. It was beautiful, *he* was beautiful, and I felt myself falling for this sexy, dangerous man, who offered me comfort and safety in a way no one else in my life ever had.

We didn't rush, instead relishing the feeling of being joined. Loving every movement, every sigh, every touch.

Reveling in the fact that we were alive.

# Chapter 31

"Thanks for coming over so quickly," I said to Carmen as I opened my door and let her inside.

I'd been back in my apartment for three days. My kids were home and we were working on getting back to normal. The first time we'd parked in the lot and walked inside, I'd watched as my kids looked warily to the place where they'd seen me snatched, but luckily, they didn't seem to be afraid to be back in our home.

"Are you kidding?" Carmen asked, bounding inside. "I was so excited to get your call that I sped the whole way here. I'm lucky I didn't get a ticket."

I chuckled at her exuberance I shut the door behind her.

"We can go in the living room or the dining room, whichever you'd prefer."

"Living room works," Carmen said, not waiting for me to show her around, instead moving down the hall on her own.

"Would you like something to drink?"

"Water would be great," she called back as she disappeared around the corner. "Great sofa."

Still chuckling, I got us both water and met her in the living room where she was already setting her stuff out on the coffee table and sitting on my couch as if she'd been over a million times before.

I sat down in the chair adjacent to the couch, watching as she laid out a notebook, pen, pencil, old-school recording device, and smart phone, all in a neat little row in front of her.

I placed her water in front of her and she promptly moved it to the right of her phone, a little bit above her neat row.

She must have noticed my little smile because she shrugged and said unapologetically, "OCD."

"So, how should we do this?" I asked, a little nervous.

"Just start at the beginning and tell me everything as if you're telling me a story. I'll record it and take notes, so I don't leave anything out and when I write it I'll make sure to hit all of the important points."

"Okay," I replied, taking a sip of my water, then a deep breath, before telling her everything.

From the cokehead to Hector, to the Coke Club and everything I'd overheard them say and do. I told her all about Moose, the case, and Carlos, and I gave her a thumb drive with copies of all of the pictures I'd taken that pertained to the case. She took down information about Bea and Cade, and said she'd try to get them to corroborate my story, but I warned her that Cade probably wouldn't be very forthcoming.

I'd spoken to Bea and the Coke Club had been arrested, Moose's body had been taken to the morgue, and they were searching for Hector and Carlos, but so far, no luck.

Bea wasn't thrilled I was speaking with the media, but I promised to only speak with Carmen and said I'd ask Carmen to run the piece by her before going to print, just to make sure it wouldn't hinder the investigation in any way.

"This is going to be awesome," Carmen gushed when I finished. "You truly are a town hero, Lila, and I cannot wait to let everyone know it." Then her grin turned wicked. "I'm honored that you and Bea trust me with this and I really look forward to exposing all of those women who thought they could make extra money by becoming drug dealers. What a bunch of assholes."

I burst out laughing, surprised, but finding I *really* liked Carmen Santos.

"What are you going to do now?" she asked, piling all of her things back into her killer handbag.

"I'm not sure yet," I replied honestly. "With Moose gone I don't have a job anymore. I love working with Amy May at the bakery, but it's just part time, which won't pay the bills … I'll come up with something, I guess."

"Well," Carmen said, her eyes on me as she rose and pulled the strap of her purse over her shoulder. "*I* think, with Moose gone, there's going to be a real need for a new PI in town."

"Yeah," I agreed. He was the only one in three counties, after all.

She looked pointedly at me … then I got it.

"Oh. What? Me? I'm not a PI. I'm not even qualified to do that."

"What do you need to do to be qualified?"

"Well, I don't know…"

"Maybe you should look into it," she suggested. "You were essentially doing all of Moose's dirty work anyway and you worked for him for over a year, right? Seems like clients wouldn't have a hard time throwing you their business."

Not really knowing how to reply, I walked her to the door in silence, my head spinning with possibilities.

"Again, thanks so much for calling me. I'm thrilled you decided to do this. I'll do you justice, I promise."

"I know you will," I replied, then added, "We'll have to set up a girl's night soon. Something involving lots of booze. We've all been dying to hear how your date went."

Carmen squealed and said, "I'd love that! But, in answer to

the dating thing, let's just say, I'm still on the market. Not everyone is lucky enough to have a random hot motorcycle man pick them up on the side of the road when they're running from drug dealers."

Another laugh burst out of me, and I thought, *I really need to keep this girl around.*

"Just sayin'," she added with a grin.

We said our goodbyes and as soon as she was gone I sent out a group text to her, Amy May, and Bea, asking when would be a good night to get together and blow off steam.

Then I went to the computer and searched: *How to be a Private Investigator.*

# Chapter 32

"Hello?" I said cautiously as I lifted my cell to my ear. The number was local but unknown and after all the hype surrounding Carmen's exposé, I'd been getting a lot of phone calls.

I don't know why I still answered...

"Delilah Horton?" a deep male voice asked.

"Yes?" I replied, ready to hang up if it was another out-of-town reporter. I'd given the only interview I planned on giving on the subject of the Chavez brothers.

"Ma'am, this is Branson Braswell, Mr. Samuel Sturgis's attorney."

"I'm sorry, you must have the wrong person. I don't know a Samuel Sturgis."

"I believe you knew him as Moose," the deep voice replied.

"*Moose?*" I asked as pain hit me in the chest at the memories hearing that name invoked.

"Yes, ma'am. I'd like to meet with you, maybe set up a time for you to come by the office?"

"The office?" I asked again, realizing I kept repeating what he said, but confused as to the nature of his call.

"Or, if you'd rather, I can come to you. Meet you wherever you'd like. I won't take up much of your time, Ms. Horton."

"Um, I'm at Jake's right now." I looked up at the clock over the bar and was about to say I could meet him in an hour, but he replied before I could.

"I'm actually just a block away, I'll be there in a minute."

I pulled my phone away from my ear and looked at it.

He'd hung up.

What a strange turn of events. I was at Jake's waiting for Cade to meet me for lunch and now I had some lawyer coming to talk to me about Moose.

*Did lawyers make house calls … or bar and grill calls, in this case?*

My life had been such a whirlwind lately I wondered how anything still managed to surprise me, but this did. What could Moose's lawyer want with me?

I sipped my diet Pepsi, eyes on the door, wondering what the lawyer would look like. The voice had been nice, but you could hardly tell by a voice on the phone how someone would look.

Expecting an older man in a vintage suit with a fifty-dollar haircut and a pot belly, I didn't immediately register that the man who'd just walked in was heading my way.

Tall and slender, but if the forearms exposed by his rolled-up shirtsleeves were any indication, very fit, with an almost military-style haircut and piercing blue eyes. The man was in dress slack, fancy shoes, and a button-up shirt, looking more like a man ready to relax at home after a long day's work than a lawyer ready to conduct business.

But when he sidled up next to me with a smile, hand outstretched, I realized that's exactly who he was.

"Branson Braswell, Ms. Horton, but you can call me Bran."

I looked from his hand to those eyes, a little tongue tied, then pulled myself out of my musings and shook his hand.

"Lila. Please, call me Lila," I replied, then gestured to the empty bar stool next to me.

Bran took his seat and when the bartender came by he asked for a water, before turning his attention back to me and asking kindly, "How are you doing, Lila? I've seen the news and read the paper, so I know you've been through an incredible ordeal. Are you holding up all right?"

It seemed strange for him to ask such a personal question, having just met me, but for some reason I knew it came from a genuine place.

Don't ask me how, just a gut feeling.

"The attention has been overwhelming, but I'm doing okay."

"Nightmares?" he asked gently, and my eyes whipped to his face.

"Yeah, how did you know?"

"I was in a similar situation as a child," Bran replied vaguely, then shifted in his seat and changed the subject. "I don't want to take up too much of your time, Lila, so I'll get right to it. As I said, I was Samuel ... eh, *Moose's*, lawyer, and I've been trying to get a hold of you to go over the contents of his will."

"You have? His will? I'm sorry, things have been crazy lately, I haven't gone through all of my messages yet." I looked down at my finger, which was making little circles on the bar, then looked up and saw that he was watching my finger as well.

"I know, that's what I figured, and I didn't want to push, but it's been a few weeks and you need to know what was in his will," Bran said patiently, and I realized his voice had a real soothing quality to it.

"Oh? Did he leave me something?" I asked lamely. *Obviously he did, or else Mr. Hot Guy Lawyer wouldn't have been leaving me messages and tracking me down in a bar.*

"Everything," he said oddly. "Moose left you everything. His house, his firm, everything…"

"*What?*" I cried, spinning on my stool so my legs bumped his as I brought my body around to face him.

Bran nodded.

"He has no family… Parents are both dead, never married, no kids. You're the closest to him."

"That's so … sad," I said softly, thinking what it would be like to have no one. Then a vision of me smashing Moose's kneecaps hit me and my hand flew to my mouth. "*Oh, my God* … But I … and he…" My eyes filled with tears.

Branson must have understood the look on my face, because his hand covered mine on the bar and he said softly, "That wasn't your fault, Lila. You were under the influence and had no control over what you were doing. Moose knew that and I know he wouldn't blame you for what happened to him. He knew fully well the kind of men he was getting involved with when he accepted Carlos Chavez as a client. Why do you think he came to me and made up that will?"

My brain was trying to make sense of everything, when I felt Bran squeeze my hand.

"If you ever want to talk … about what happened, or anything at all, just give me a call," Bran said, eyes intent so I couldn't mistake his meaning.

I was about to respond when I felt a large, warm arm hit my shoulder and Cade's gruff voice say, "She's good."

I looked up to see Cade glaring down at Bran, then turned to see Branson grin and lift up one shoulder.

"You can't blame a man for trying, Wilkes."

Cade continued to glare and replied, "As long as it only happens once."

I looked from Cade, his long dark hair wild and unruly around his scowling face, to Bran, who was handsome in a casual, clean-cut way, and was grinning madly at Cade's scowl, totally unperturbed and wondered how in the hell I'd gone from taking an impromptu snapshot of my cheating ex to this moment right here.

Branson rose from his stool and laid his business card on the bar in front of me, then threw down enough money to cover my drink and a tip and said, "Call me and we'll set up a time for you to come down to the office, sign the papers, and make everything official."

"Okay, thanks, Bran, I will," I responded with a smile, then watched him tilt his chin to Cade and walk away.

"What was that all about?" I asked Cade as he took Branson's vacated seat.

"I think it's time for me to meet your kids," Cade said, causing my heart to stutter in my chest. "You guys could come over this Saturday, we can cook out, they can play with Rufus."

I sat there, mouth gaping like a fish, with no words coming out.

*He wants to meet my kids? Are we moving too fast? Am I ready to take that next step with him?*

"Darlin'," Cade whispered, leaning forward, head bent to mine. "We've got a good thing here."

I tilted my head back and nodded, then said, "I need a cupcake."

Cade's grin spread wide, making his dangerously beautiful face even more so, and replied, "Then, let's go get my woman a cupcake."

# Chapter 33

"This is what I'm talking about!" I shouted to my friends, trying to be heard over the loud music as we walked through the crowd of people in the club.

We were finally out for a much-needed girl's night. This time, not just dinner and drinks, but an actual, out after ten PM, night on the town, *girl's night*.

Amy May looked sweet in a pair of short black shorts and a shimmery silver top, her shoulder-length, dirty-blonde hair falling in finger waves around her face. Bea had gone for an edgier look, her dark pixie cut spiked up, wearing tight leather pants and a kick-ass black vest. Carmen had her caramel-and-blonde hombre piled high on top of her head with a few loose tendrils framing her face, her toned body on display in a sexy mini-dress.

I grinned happily, slightly buzzed from my pre-game festivities while getting decked out in my navy-blue shorts with large buttons accenting the top and a silky white camisole. My auburn hair was falling in loose, natural waves down my back, and I had fabulous navy wedges on my feet. Painful, but fabulous.

We hit the bar, knocked back a couple shots, then headed for the dance floor.

Dancing happily, I looked at my friends, then at the crowd around us, noticing that for a group of women in our thirties, we had a number of eyes on us as we danced in our circle. We looked good and we were working it…

After a few songs, Amy May gave the international sign for *let's get a drink* and we all moved back toward the bar. Once we had drinks in hand, we maneuvered through the crush of people, Bea in the lead, until we were walking down the hall and into one of the back rooms. The music was quieter in here and rather than a dance floor, it was filled with pool tables, high top tables, and a few lush couches and chairs making up different sitting areas.

We were lucky to snag a grouping of chairs in the back corner of the room.

"So," Bea started as we sat, her face flush with something more than exertion, then took a sip of her red wine before looking at each of us and saying, "I've decided when Shannon and I go to the beach this summer for vacation, I'm going to ask her to marry me."

"What?" I screamed, jumping up out of my seat in excitement and knocking my nearly full dirty martini over.

"*Party foul,*" some guy from the table next to us yelled, but I ignored him and happy danced all the way to Bea, putting my hands on her shoulders and jumping up and down in front of her while she looked up at me, laughing.

"I'm so happy for you," I said, stating the obvious as I leaned down and gave her a big, loud kiss on the lips.

"*Yeah,*" the same guy shouted, and this time I shot him a death glare before giving her shoulders a squeeze and bounding back to my seat.

"I tried to save it," Carmen said, handing me my empty

cup, before turning to Bea and asking, "How long have you two been together?"

Bea leaned back from Amy May's congratulatory hug and replied, "Three years."

"Wow, three years, that's awesome. Congratulations."

"How are things going with you and Jason?" Bea asked, never one to want to be the center of attention for too long. "Go on any sexy dates lately?"

I gasped, then looked at Amy May, whose eyes were narrowed on me.

"Someone has a big mouth," she said, but gave away that she wasn't mad when her lips turned up. "And, no, not since Lila caught us in the act," she laughed and added, "But I did get a new wig the other day, so I'll need to try it on soon."

"Ooooh, what do you need wigs for?" Carmen asked, leaning closer to Amy May as she lifted her Appletini to her lips.

"My husband and I like to spice things up by role playing."

"Yeah," I said, really wishing I hadn't spilled my drink. "They go out on dates, acting like strangers and dressing up, then go home together and have one-night stands. She's such a floozy."

"That sounds *amazing*," Carmen cooed. "I love that you're keeping your relationship fresh like that … aww."

"How are things with Cade?" Amy May asked, turning the table on me.

Just the sound of his name had my body warming more than alcohol ever could. I looked at her dreamily and said, "Soooo good." Then I remembered our conversation yesterday and I bit my lip nervously and told my friends, "He wants to meet the kids."

Bea's face showed her surprise.

"Really? He's ready for that? Are you?"

I thought about Cade, what I knew about him and everything we'd been through since we met and said, "Yeah, I think I am. I've never met anyone like him, never had anyone make me feel so safe, and at the same time, so *wanted* ... I think he'll be in my life for a long time, so yeah, the kids should meet him."

"They're going to love him," Amy May said, "Especially Elin."

I grinned at the thought of my son and the motorcycle badass in question. She was right, Elin was going to think he was the *coolest* guy ever. I actually couldn't wait to see how Cade interacted with my children.

"Wow," Carmen said again, this time wistfully. "You guys are all so lucky, to have found these amazing people to share your life with. I always seem to attract losers and criminals. I'd give anything to have a relationship like yours."

"Your date with Mr. Hoodie didn't go so well?" Bea asked.

Carmen shook her head and said with a sigh, "No, you were right about him."

I reached over and grabbed Carmen's hand in mine, waiting until her eyes found mine before assuring her, "You're going to find the right guy for you, I promise. You may have to sift through a few losers first, but, Carmen, you're a total catch, it'll happen. You just have to wait for the right one."

"Totally," Amy May agreed.

"Yup, just be patient," Bea added, "And, *picky*."

"Thanks, guys," Carmen said, her happy smile back. "I'm so happy you invited me along."

"Of course," I said, "This is the first of many good times to come. Now, who else needs another drink?"

Amy May said she'd join me and as I walked the room, hand in hand with my best friend, I realized my life was better now than it had ever been before and I couldn't wait to see what happened next.

# Epilogue

My heart was in my throat as Cade's log cabin came in to view. Elena took in a sharp breath and Elin exclaimed, *"No way,* is that his house?"

I chuckled as I looked in the rearview mirror and took in my son's face.

"Yeah, buddy, that's his house."

*"Cool."*

"Is that him?" Elena asked, and I looked to the side of the house to see Cade standing there, watching the van come up the drive with Rufus sitting beside him.

"Yes."

"Wow," my daughter breathed.

His hair down and still wet from his shower, it looked ink black and was starting to curl slightly. His beard looked trimmed, but paired with his very long, very large body, the well-worn jeans, and leather vest over a simple gray T-shirt, he was a sexy, but imposing sight.

For the first time I worried that they'd be afraid of him, due to his presence and stature alone, but when I saw Elin watching him in awe and Elena gazing at him curiously, I figured they were going to be just fine.

The fact that they loved dogs would only help in their transition.

I pulled next to his truck and parked. Elin was out the door before I'd even gotten the key out of the ignition. Elena was a little shyer, so she waited for me, taking my hand and walking next to me as we watched Elin go straight for Rufus. Hitting his knees as soon as he was close enough, Elin wrapped his arms around Rufus's neck and the two instantly fell in love.

Cade was watching the pair, a small smile playing on his lips, then brought his gaze to my daughter.

"You must be Elena," he said gruffly, holding out his hand.

Elena looked up at me, then down at her brother and Rufus, before finally looking Cade cautiously in the eye and placing her small hand in his large one.

He turned it, bending low as he brought their hands to his lips and kissed the back of her hand lightly.

Elena giggled, as any woman being wooed by a dangerous man would, and said, "Your beard tickles," then she dropped to hug Rufus herself.

"Hey," I said once both kids were occupied with the dog and was surprised when Cade moved to me and kissed me softly before grinning down at me.

"Hey."

My eyes shot nervously to my kids, who were watching us with wide eyes, then Elin looked Cade over and said, "You wear a lot of jewelry for a man."

"*Elin*," I chastised, but Cade just laughed and gave my hand a reassuring squeeze.

"Yeah, little brother, I do." Then he crouched down and lifted his necklace.

Both of my kids leaned in, fascinated by him. Elin even rested his hand on Cade's raised knee. "See this, it's a shark tooth. My father gave it to me last time I was home. This ring," he said, lifting one pinkie, "is from my mother. She said the stone will always keep me safe and help me live a balanced life. This one," he raised his other pinkie, "is from my sister. She gave it to me for Christmas three years ago. And this." He spread his hand and pointed to the large skull ring. "That one I bought because I thought it kicked ass."

Elin laughed at the swear word, then looked nervously up at me. I just rolled my eyes and shook my head, letting him know he probably shouldn't tell Cade he owed money to the swear jar. At least not at their first meeting.

Elena was still watching him with avid interest.

"Where's home?" she asked, catching on to the fact that if he was going home, his family obviously didn't live here.

"Hawaii," Cade answered as he rose back up.

"Cool," Elin said again, and I had a feeling I'd be hearing that word a lot out of my son that day.

"Mom," Elena said, her little brain working quickly as usual. "Since Cade's your boyfriend, does that mean we'll get to go to Hawaii?"

"No, sweetheart," I replied, at the same time Cade said, "Absolutely."

I looked up at him, surprised and asked, "Really?"

"Yeah, darlin'," Cade replied, reaching a hand out to cup my jaw sweetly. "My family likes me to visit, especially during the holidays and I know they'll want to meet you and the twins."

Excitement filled me at the thought of traveling to Hawaii, a place I'd always wanted to go but had never been; at the same time the thought of meeting Cade's family freaked me the hell out.

Seeing the panic in my eyes he said, "They'll love you, Lila, believe me. My mom has been waiting for me to bring a woman home since I was old enough to vote. Bringing home you *and* two awesome kids? She'll be in heaven."

I looked down and saw my kids faces soften at the compliment, then they began to hop around and chant, "*We're going to Hawaii, we're going to Hawaii,*" as they danced around the yard with Rufus in tow.

*Oh yeah*, I thought, *life is pretty damn sweet.*

Keep reading for a look at
book 2, Cupcake Overload!

# Prologue ~ Cupcake Overload

One night I was out with my girls, enjoying a much-needed ladies' night while wondering if one more dirty martini would push me over the edge. The next thing I knew we were in the middle of a situation that no group of mostly drunk women should be in.

It started when Bea said she needed to use the restroom, which led to Amy May saying she was about to burst, and Carmen and I deciding we might as well all go so we could head back out onto the dance floor as soon as possible.

It was just our luck that from the stall in the back we heard a woman screaming "*No*" and a man's voice telling her, "*I know you want it.*"

That asshole picked the wrong restroom, in the wrong club, at the wrong time.

Little did I know he was Cade's VP. And, although we saved her from his clutches that night, a month later, she'd be found floating in a motel pool ... which would cause the first bit of adversity Cade and I would have to face as a couple.

*Well, that and Branson Braswell.*

Who would have thought I'd miss the days where my biggest problem was my cheating, douchebag ex?

Running a PI firm was a lot harder than taking pictures for one, especially when your professional life spilled over into your personal one. And dating an alpha male who rode a motorcycle and looked good doing it wasn't always sunshine and roses.

I was going through cupcakes like our new puppy went through piddle pads and if I wasn't careful there would be a *Cupcake Overload*.

# Acknowledgments

Thanks to Lori and Ann for reading Cupcakes while it was still in the "Can I really write this book?" stage. Your input was great, and your enthusiasm for the characters really helped fuel me along.

Thanks to S.L. Scott, for looking over the first few chapters and giving me some input. It really meant a lot!

To Jennifer, Lyn, Michelle, Chloe, and Autumn for Beta reading and helping me make the story better.

Kristina and Karen for agreeing to edit and format on short notice, because I was so excited about the book I didn't want to wait too long to get it out to the readers. I love you both so hard!

Allie. Oh, Allie, I owe you so much more than thanks, and really hope we get to meet in person some day. You're covers are always so beautiful, and yet you still listen to my thoughts and answer my questions, even though you always end up being right in the end. Thanks for having so much patience with me!

To Jaime, for supporting me over the last five years of this crazy journey, and for always believing in me. And to our kids, for giving me the space to realize my dream, and for pulling me back to reality when I need it.

# About the Author

Bethany Lopez is a USA Today Bestselling author of more than forty books and has been published since 2011. She's a lover of all things romance, which she incorporates into the books she writes, no matter the genre.

When she isn't reading or writing, she loves spending time with family and traveling whenever possible.

Bethany can usually be found with a cup of coffee or glass of wine at hand, and will never turn down a cupcake!

To learn more about upcoming events and releases, sign up for my newsletter.

www.bethanylopezauthor.com
bethanylopezauthor@gmail.com

*Follow her at* https://www.bookbub.com/authors/bethany-lopez *to get an alert whenever she has a new release, preorder, or discount!*

Also by Bethany Lopez

**Contemporary Romance:**

*The Jilted Wives Club Trilogy*

Starter Wife

Trophy Wife

Work Wife

Backup Wife - Preorder Now

Accidental Wife

*Mason Creek Series*

Perfect Summer

Perfect Christmas Anthology - Coming Soon

Perfect Hideaway - Coming Soon

Perfect Fall - Coming Soon

*A Time for Love Series*

Prequel - 1 Night - FREE

8 Weeks - FREE

21 Days

42 Hours

15 Minutes

10 Years

3 Seconds

7 Months

For Eternity - Novella

Night & Day - Novella

Time for Love Series Box Set

Time to Risk

## *The Lewis Cousins Series (KU)*

Too Tempting

Too Complicated

Too Distracting

Too Enchanting

Too Dangerous

The Lewis Cousins Box Set

Too Enticing - Short

## *Three Sisters Catering Trilogy*

A Pinch of Salt

A Touch of Cinnamon

A Splash of Vanilla

Three Sisters Catering Trilogy Box Set

## *Frat House Confessions*

Frat House Confessions: Ridge

Frat House Confessions: Wes

Frat House Confessions: Brody

Frat House Confessions 1 - 3 Box Set

Frat House Confessions: Crush - Coming Soon

## **Romantic Comedy/Suspense:**
## *Delilah Horton Series*

Always Room for Cupcakes - FREE

Cupcake Overload

Lei'd with Cupcakes

Cupcake Explosion

Cupcakes & Macaroons - Honeymoon Short - FREE

Lei'd in Paradise - Novella (Carmen & Bran)

Crazy for Cupcakes - Coming Soon

## Women's Fiction:

More than Exist

Unwoven Ties

## Short Stories/Novellas:

*Contemporary:*

Christmas Come Early

Harem Night

Reunion Fling

An Inconvenient Dare

Snowflakes & Country Songs

Fool for You - FREE

Desert Alpha (Lady Boss Press Navy SEAL Novella)

*Fantasy:*

Leap of Faith

Beau and the Beastess

## Cookbook:

Love & Recipes

Love & Cupcakes

**Children's:**

Katie and the North Star

**Young Adult:**

*Stories about Melissa – series*

Ta Ta for Now!

xoxoxo

Ciao

TTYL

Stories About Melissa Books 1 - 4

With Love

Adios

**Young Adult Fantasy:**

Nissa: a contemporary fairy tale

**New Adult:**

*Friends & Lovers Trilogy*

Make it Last

I Choose You

Trust in Me

Indelible

Made in the USA
Las Vegas, NV
10 September 2024